THE MEANING OF IF

Also by Patrick Lawler

Fiction

Rescuers of Skydivers Search Among the Clouds

Poetry

A Drowning Man Is Never Tall Enough
reading a burning book
Feeding the Fear of the Earth
Trade World Center
Underground (Notes Toward an Autobiography)
Child Sings in the Womb

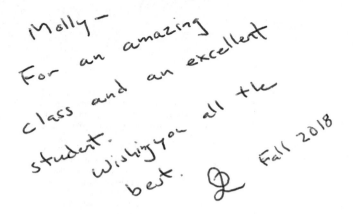

Molly —
For an amazing
class and an excellent
student. Wishing you all the
best. _P_ Fall 2018

THE MEANING OF IF

Patrick Lawler

Patrick Lawler

Four Way Books

Tribeca

Please direct all inquiries to:
Editorial Office
Four Way Books
POB 535, Village Station
New York, NY 10014
www.fourwaybooks.com

Library of Congress Cataloging-in-Publication Data

Lawler, Patrick.
[Short stories. Selections]
The meaning of if / by Patrick Lawler.
pages cm
ISBN 978-1-935536-45-1 (alk. paper)
I. Title.
PS3562.A867M43 2014
813'.54--dc23
                                  2013036095

This book is manufactured in the United States of America and printed on acid-free paper.

Four Way Books is a not-for-profit literary press. We are grateful for the assistance
we receive from individual donors, public arts agencies, and private foundations.

State of the Arts

NYSCA

This publication is made possible with public funds from
the New York State Council on the Arts, a state agency.

[clmp]

We are a proud member
of the Council of Literary Magazines and Presses.

Distributed by University Press of New England
One Court Street, Lebanon, NH 03766

CONTENTS

For

my daughter and son-in-law—

Nicole and Ryan.

And especially for

my grandson—Dylan Patrick.

May you discover the richness of If and the

Meaningfulness in all that you touch and

all that touches you.

Patrick Lawler

THE MEANING OF IF

After lengthy negotiations, Minister Blakely, old and wobbly, acquired the right to use my grandfather's yard for burials. In return, my grandfather and his heirs were allowed the use of the house without rent or mortgage for three generations, provided with free burial for three generations, and given a tidy sum of money that my grandfather promptly spent in a three-day celebration to commemorate his outwitting the Minister Blakely.

It wasn't long before the first hole was dug, and the body of Wilbur F. Chase, the owner of the local hardware store, was lowered into it. My father, who worked with my grandfather as a house painter, was washing out some brushes in the sink, the paint swirling out of the bristles in rainbows. "I don't know about this deal," he said to my grandfather, who was sitting at the kitchen table with me. My grandfather's hands were always a milky white from his having cleaned them too much with gasoline, while my father's hands changed pigment almost every week, depending on the colors he was using on the job. The black cars pulled up like something coming into consciousness, and my mother timidly leaned into the kitchen curtains, waved some hair out of her eyes, turned to my grandfather, and turned back to the black of the cars. She wasn't pleased with this new arrangement. I was sitting across from my grandfather, shuffling some paint samples.

"He's been dying a long time," my father said, rubbing his nut-colored hands. "Last time I was down there to get some nails, he was shaking so badly he could hardly put them in the bag."

"It's true. Never spill a bag of nails. Inside, at least. That's what they say. And if you do, you must use them immediately," my mother said, still looking out the window.

"Would've been pounding those things for weeks."

"Could have made his own coffin," said Grandfather. "Never really thought he'd do it."

He never really thought Minister Blakely would bury people in his front lawn. "They're almost finished," my mother said, and she took a thin, brownish towel from her shoulder and began wiping the dishes. My father worked the old stubby brushes until the black bristles glistened.

"Let's not think about the past," my grandfather said. "There's no future in it. The deal's fine. For us it's fine. Remember: three generations. Me, you, and your boy over there." He pointed at me and I looked down at the paint samples. I flicked through them. Five different rectangles of blue on each one. Five different windows. Six different cards. Thirty different skies. "For us it's fine, and at least for now we're all there is."

Soon Emmett Boggs (1891–1975) joined Wilbur F. Chase. And then Katherine Bickle (1921–1976) and Walter M. Mann (1906–1976). And Margaret (his wife) joined Wilbur. And R. C. Look and Larry Coons. Otis (1910–1977) joined Katherine. Emmett Boggs's last name was misspelled on the stone so that it read "Emmett Baggs." This was only the first in a series of unfortunate events, which included Margaret (wife of Wilbur F.) being put in the plot of Mary (wife of Walter M.). Mary never got over this.

One day some men came and put up a black iron fence, and there was a black crooked gate in front of the house with dark letters arcing over the gate:

THE MEANING OF LIFE CEMETERY

Though changes had to be made in our lives, my two sisters and I easily adapted to the surroundings. I played in the garage with the cans of shellac, linseed oil, and gum turpentine, the paint paddles with thick bands of color, the wooden ladders, the color-splotched drop cloths. My sisters played tag, twirling around the headstones, my mother yelling, "How many times must I tell you? Leave Wilbur Chase alone." Saturday funerals were the worst: we had to be quiet. The dark cars sailed toward us out of the bleary sunlight; my mother, hanging clothes over the headstones, would silently disappear into the house. And the new minister, Robert Barth, a young man with a straight back and stiff lips, would mumble words that would click over his teeth, around the stones, and through the kitchen window. We tried to stay quiet, at my mother's request, as if one small ripple of laughter would capsize the whole solemn event. And people always cried at certain parts. Always. And we would hear them crying through the closed glass of the kitchen window.

They became as familiar as our relatives: Emmett and Katherine and Wilbur and R.C. and then Robert Himpler (1929–1978) and Claire

The Meaning of If

Gluck (1868–1978) and Mrs. Jonathan B. Sudds (1903–1979), the wife of the doctor. And then my grandfather.

Dr. Sudds said it was something growing inside him. Though my grandfather never explained why, he blamed Minister Blakely. During the last days, my grandfather did nothing but grow. He seemed not to mind his impending death and actually seemed to accept it, which my mother said was healthy, considering the situation. He refused to eat or leave the bed. Or move or look or talk or smile. He just lay there, his painter's cap dipped on the bedpost, his spotted shoes tucked under a chair. Because of my grandfather's decision not to do *anything,* there was the problem of identifying the moment when he died. My mother had the solution. She would touch the flame of a candle to the tip of one of his great toes. A blister would rise. "If he is dead," she said, "the blister will be full of air and will burst noisily when, for a second time, the flame is applied. If he is alive, the blister will not burst." My father wasn't impressed, but added that he wasn't about to come up with anything better.

My grandfather's hands went from a milky white to a silver, and then one day the blister burst. Because my father had just finished painting the cemetery gate, his hands were black. After my mother covered all the mirrors in the house with old sheets she pulled out of her closet, she wept into the shoulder of my father, his black hands caressing her hair. Later, Grandfather's stone was placed next to the porch.

After the funeral, my father wouldn't allow me to forget the bargain struck by his father. "You'll be the last. Remember that. The last."

We became more and more comfortable with the idea of the cemetery. For picnics we used the headstones instead of lawn furniture, and my father spread a plank between Willy Crofut and Emmett Boggs's headstone—and we had ourselves a table. Neighbors and relatives, although at first cautious, began to approach the subject casually. When Mrs. Dun, a close friend of my mother, would come over to eat donuts, she called it her "coffin break," and she'd laugh weirdly into her sugar-sprinkled napkin. As the little mats of shadows fell behind each stone, my sisters placed their plastic tea set in the front of Claire Gluck and invited her to tea. The alder trees and the linden trees swayed like heavy aunts, and the willows drooped.

As I grew, life became more complicated, and the yard only reflected that complication. More died and people brought bright-red coffee cans filled with flowers, and my father cleaned his brushes in them when he came home from work. The school bus dragged itself through the winter streets, the thick, brushed-on clouds of winter hanging over the house: in the hot summers the days stuck together; and in the autumn the raw leaves, the chewed leaves, clung to the base of the stones. All year long, people asked each other why the flowers in the cemetery always died.

After high school graduation, my father wrapped his blue hands around mine, and I went to work with him painting houses. For the most part, I prepared them; I scraped and sanded and wire brushed and primed. At first he had me paint the less-conspicuous areas—a garage, a shed—while he left the tricky parts for himself. But as the summer passed, that changed: I became more and more adept at handling a brush. (My father would never allow me to use anything smaller than a three-inch brush for even the smallest of areas.)

In the middle of September, Mary Mann said she had some rental property she wanted my father to paint. It was a two-family house near the county line, about a mile from the community college. "Don't charge me a lot," she said. "I don't want you wasting your time scraping and all that. Just slap the cheapest stuff you got on it, and I'll be happy." My father had principles, but, when money was involved, he wasn't reluctant to change them. We began painting the two-family house and I met Karla.

I was on the ladder, painting the soffit, when I first saw her going into the house. Later, I learned she lived there with two others who were attending the local college. She offered me a drink once when it was rather warm, and I began to take breaks when she was around. She always had cat hair clinging to her clothes and smelled like ketchup, for, though she had attended college, she had dropped out and was working as a waitress.

"I love to paint, too," Karla said. My father told her that things were slow in the fall, but if he had any work, he would keep her in mind. Later, she took me into her bedroom and showed me canvases of oil paintings. They seemed rather sensual, but that could have been the cats that rubbed against my legs or the pillows or the puffy slippers or the tiny piles of clothes I knew I shouldn't have been looking at.

"That's what I went to school for."

"What?"

"Art."

I didn't want to say it, but it did seem apparent that she hadn't finished.

Sometimes I would be at the frosted window of the bathroom, scraping away at some loose putty, or I'd be at her bedroom window with the shade drawn, painting the sash. I'd realize that all the windows of the house had been painted shut with decades and decades of paint, and I'd feel Karla's presence behind the windows. Maybe she would be dipping a skinny brush into a smudge of paint. Maybe she would be slipping into the powder-blue outfit she wore when she went to work.

After the job was done, we still saw each other. We would make love in front of the weird paintings, with cats moving around our feet and over our hips, a tail swishing Karla's nipples. At the end of the semester, her housemates went away to four-year schools, and Karla and I got married.

We moved into the Meaning of Life Cemetery, where she was introduced to Wilbur Chase, Robert Himpler, and Mrs. Jonathan B. Sudds. The cats belonged to Karla, and they came with her, along with a number of canvases. My mother felt that this was a little too much. "Don't you feel the house is a bit small?" she asked. The cats were named Raphael, Rubens, Renoir, Gauguin, Goya, Picasso, Chagall, Botticelli, and Van Gogh. I had intended to convey my mother's reservations, but Karla said, "You know, Gauguin always reminds me of you."

At first, Karla seemed to enjoy the occasions when the hearse would pull up to the side of the house. I suppose *enjoy* is not the right word, but she never seemed to mind it. Sitting in the front yard with an easel arranged in front of her, she painted pictures with titles like "Picasso and Renoir Hiding Behind a Stone" or "Goya Sleeping." She loved the stones: the roughly hewn rectangles, the smooth-finished cream trapezoidal stones, the green marble, the simple elegance of the inscriptions:

Nancy
Wife of
Wm. Baldwin
Died

The Meaning of If

In

Memory of

John Bender

The house was packed with people and cats, and my father couldn't keep his truck in the garage anymore because of the bags of kitty litter and cat food, the paint cans and ladders, and the bundles of lumpy stiff drop cloths. Except for my youngest sister, Nicole, who was allergic to cats and who would hide their bowls of milk, my family came to accept Karla, and even love her.

At night, Picasso curled cloud-like in her lap.

For awhile it didn't seem as if anyone was dying, and the house grew quiet. Only my father's truck clunked up the macadam drive that curved past the stones and toward our front porch. My sisters moved into adolescence like butterflies, and then Becky was eighteen and about to get married to Wilbur F. Chase's grandson, Buddy.

"But I've always dreamed of a garden wedding," she said.

"We don't have a garden. Not now, at least," said my mother.

"It's just not right," protested Becky.

Always wanting to please his oldest daughter, my father said, "Damn it, Becky. If that's what you want, that's what we'll have."

The preparations began. My father dragged out his drop cloths with the hardened drops of paint sprinkled over them. He and I draped them over the headstones, while my mother and Nicole made flower arrangements to place on top of them. All the stones were covered except my grandfather's. An archway was made from two broken ladders, and Karla painted a picture called "Raphael at the Wedding Feast."

The day arrived. Everyone was there except Mary Mann, who refused to come to the cemetery after the mistake with her husband's plot. Reverend Barth was there. My youngest sister and Karla were in the wedding party. It was a sparkling day. Rubens clung to the legs of chairs, Chagall floated among the shoes of the wedding guests, and Botticelli drifted like breath to the tables filled with food. My father gave Becky away, his hands a pale, pale blue. Later my mother kissed Becky, and then kissed Buddy.

In bed that night, Karla told me she was pregnant. Due in January. Did you see Dr. Sudds? He said January. Great. Great. I love you. Love you. I can't tell you how much I . . .

I was ecstatic. I seemed to drift on the ladders—scraping and wire brushing and priming, all in one easy motion. The four-inch brush glided over the houses: the soffits, the facia, the window sashes fell into new colors.

The jobs blew by.

We painted the restaurant a meaty red color.

We painted the bar where my grandfather had celebrated after the deal with Minister Blakely.

We painted the hardware store, which was going to be sold because Buddy's father had had a stroke after running a sale on shovels.

And the colors never came out of my hands. The violets and pinks and greens. The mint colors and the trim colors. The disturbing yellows.

During the summer months, the cemetery came to life: lawn mowers gargled between headstones, and teenagers drank six-packs on the hot nights. The man who took care of the cemetery clipped the grass and dug, unless there was a funeral, and then he would stand off to one side, hiding his shovel.

So the world seemed full of meaningful activity as Karla advanced in her pregnancy. Everything mattered; everything was connected.

My mother asked me if anything was wrong and I said no but I didn't know if I meant it.

In October, Karla announced she was going to work on her last painting. "Can you let me use one of your father's old drop cloths? It will be perfect." It was sprinkled with white dots from rolling ceilings and had some red cut across it from doing the doorway of the restaurant. There was a big yellow splatter like a sun. "It'll be perfect."

She called the painting "Van Gogh and the Meaning of Life." She stayed up very late at night and worked in the poor light of the basement, cats jumping around her feet or sprawling on the old pool table with the ripped felt or sleeping behind canning jars. They'd pad their way around her, leap and land. Picasso sat like a quart of porch paint. The old drop cloth, which had been stretched with pieces of two-inch pine, was laid across six sawhorses. Karla was bent over a corner of it.

"My mother thinks there is something wrong here," I said.

"You can't feel it, can you?" Her brush swirled something the color of rotten leaves. "You can't feel me moving through these layers and layers."

"I am happy," I said. "Shouldn't I be?"

"I suppose."

"Is there something wrong with me? It's the cemetery, isn't it? We can move. We will—"

"No. No." Van Gogh idled in a corner. "I'm being squeezed and nothing's coming out. I don't understand what is happening, but I must allow it to happen. And so must you."

Karla was always convinced she was going to have a son. "What kind of a name is Chase?" asked my father. His hands were the color of eggshells.

After Chase was born, Karla said she had to leave. Because all of this only exists now as echo, I'm not even certain the words were said.

All we have around us is destination.

I suppose. . . . But it's not that bad knowing where you're going.

I don't want to already be where I'm going. That's the point.

Do you love me?

That's not the point.

Why?

It's not you. It's not your family. It's me.

What about . . .

I've got to.

The car floated ahead of its exhaust and drifted under the tiny letters arcing over the gate. The *L* and *E* had long since vanished, from either rust or vandals. My hands carried the colors of all the houses in the town. The cats arched and scratched, always hungry. They were walking secrets, rumors with paws. Without Karla, they became indolent, surreptitious. Picasso looked stepped on. Their tails turned into shoelaces. They scratched and scratched. Their odd hungry music filled the house. They licked themselves until they vanished.

That spring I began painting with my father again. My hands carried all the colors of the town.

The Meaning of If

Tobacco brown

and

Hickory.

Sylvan green

and

Fawn.

Melon,

Mint,

and

Dresden blue.

Bone white.

Linen white.

Spanish white.

China white.

Cherry,

Celery,

Silk,

and

Sky.

Apricot

and

Midnight plum.

Black. And blacker black.

My mother was very upset and refused to have Karla's name mentioned by my two remaining sisters. "Why? You shouldn't allow her to set foot back in this house. Not with the way she treated you. Never.

Your father wouldn't, believe me. Of course, I wouldn't either. I mean, I wouldn't have done what she did."

My father said: *It's too bad it really is I mean you know talk to me if you have to I know what you must be going through but then again I don't and*

I often thought that I should leave—to look for her or look for Chase. But I didn't. And I wondered why she had left, but I wouldn't have been able to ask her.

More mistakes were made in the cemetery. One of the headstones read "Martha Comstock," but she didn't die. She even wanted my father and me to paint her kitchen.

Older now, Nicole, who had been allergic to the cats, put away the cats' dishes for the last time. Later I found out my mother had been saving clippings from the newspaper. They were meant for Karla. "When she comes back, she'll want to know what's been going on."

The painting Karla had worked on when she was pregnant remained in our cellar until my father, having more inside work, found himself short of drop cloths. "Would you mind?" he asked. "Do you think *she* would?"

I walked into Martha Comstock's kitchen with an extra paint pan and a gallon of ceiling paint. My father was two rungs up the stepladder, which had been stretched over Karla's canvas with the white dots, a red cut, and a big yellow splatter. And mixed into this were purples and greens and lumps of brown. Layers and layers. A floating. A churning. A bubbling. A blue breath, a stroke of sky, a crust of brown. A burrowing. Faces. Everyone was there: Emmett and Katherine and Margaret and Otis and Larry and Robert and Claire. My grandfather with his milky white hands. And Chase was behind it all, buried in the plum colors and the crimson and the aching blue. First to step foot into this new world.

I watched my father coming down the ladder. I wanted to stop him. I wanted to join him. Coming down from the ladder, my father sank into what was waiting below.

Patrick Lawler

MUSIC FOR A LADY SLEEPING IN JAPAN

My father was a virtuoso of vanishing. In World War II he had been a Japanese prisoner of war, but he had forgotten everything about the experience. He never knew if he had been tortured, if he had revealed any secrets, if he had collaborated with the enemy. The only thing that he could remember was this dream he had had about a lady sleeping in Japan.

My mother was a vital woman who had five children and an assortment of hobbies and interests that kept her occupied. But one interest began to predominate in her life: her love of Japanese art. When she brought home a Ma Yuan print, which she had found at a garage sale, she asked my father how he liked it. He studied the light and fluid lines, the texture of the Chinese black ink, the mistiness and the emptiness, and he said, "It looks as if someone is losing his hair."

At the time there were always blackouts in the village. The power company would send out formal letters of apology and offer a variety of explanations: a transformer struck by lightning, a malfunctioning turbine, sabotage by a small, disruptive group of dissidents, divine intervention. We lived with the inconvenience for awhile, but the mayor decided something had to be done, even if the blackouts *were* divinely inspired.

My mother wanted my youngest sister to study the flute. All over the house there were squeaky sounds, as if someone were squashing tiny animals. Later my father asked her to compose some original music for the lady sleeping in Japan. After my sister was finished, my father said, "Yes, that's perfect. Don't ever forget it. I may want you to play it again sometime." My mother said that she would not pay for any more flute lessons and told my sister to take up dancing.

The town came up with a solution to our problem with the power company. When the lights refused to come on, we put a match to the fattest man, after dousing him with kerosene, and had him run through the village. He would be invited into various homes. Some men would read Flaubert by his burning, some elderly women would crochet by his burning, and some children would dance around his burning. Eventually he'd go out, and we'd find another—usually a volunteer.

Some years passed. I was entering college at the time, to major in journalism. My mother began to study Zen. She would say things like "We cannot know the mind with the mind" or "To awaken is to know no." My mother continued to fill the house with artifacts from Japan. Wind chimes tinkled on our back porch, or sometimes we could hear the bamboo cluck. My father tolerated it but it pained him too, watching the culture of his captors preserved around him. He hated it when the wind blew.

Once upon a time, the woman who desired and desired and desired more was lying in bed. She wanted to weep she was so happy . . .

I met Celeste in college, and we decided that we would be married. She asked me what my father did for a living, but I could not answer her.

Patrick Lawler

Was he an electrician? A sales representative for a tool-and-die company? An executive for an investing firm? A consultant? An engineer? I had forgotten to ask him. I told Celeste that he was a virtuoso of vanishing, and she was quite pleased.

My father would sometimes disappear for days. He attributed it to his dreamy nature, but my mother announced, after she drew us children around her, "He's not fooling me. He's having an affair." An incredible sadness fell over the house. Even when the burning man was invited in, his flames only illuminated our sad, sunken faces. My youngest sister wept for days and buried her flute in the backyard.

"You might wonder why I've called you all together," the stranger said, "but I know who the murderer is."

"No one has been murdered," we protested. But we could not dissuade him. It didn't really seem to matter, he informed us. He said that nothing was to disrupt the drama of this moment, the culmination of all his efforts, the ultimate challenge to his powers of ratiocination.

My father said, "I've read nothing of a murder in the papers."

The stranger, with certainty in the tone of his voice, responded, "Don't believe everything you don't read."

My mother recited a poem by Ryōkan:

> The thief
> Left it behind—
> The moon at the window.

A wrinkle scribbled its way across the stranger's forehead.

My mother continued to decipher her koans: Hui-neng's "Original Face," Chao-chou's "Wu," and Hakuin's "One Hand." She performed tasks about the house, but we knew that behind these empty activities was her quest for the original nothing. I never asked myself, what was the sound of one hand clapping? I never pursued my original face until now.

It was not until after I graduated from college that genuine happiness returned to my family's house. I announced that I was going to work for the town's newspaper and that Celeste and I were going to be married.

My father confided in me after I returned from my honeymoon. "I am not having an affair. Maybe I'm losing my mind, but I am not having an affair. If I were, there wouldn't be a problem. I'd end it." He looked so much older, defeated, disturbed. I told him that I would help him if I could, that I really wanted to. He said, "I'm dreaming again about the sleeping lady of Japan."

Even though my mother suspected that he was having an affair, she was not really mad at my father. She kept saying things like "Though we try to avoid them, all things are present."

The stranger's name was Jeremiah Stump, but to us he always remained the stranger. He was a grubby, grizzled man, who wore a grayish-white shirt with a safety pin where a button should have been. Often he would stop by my family's house to inform the family of his progress, and sometimes he'd even stop to see Celeste and me. He once said, "Everyone refuses to remember, but I can't forget. The blood. The red, red blood."

The first year of my marriage was delirious. I enjoyed my job, and Celeste and I were totally in love. We'd lie in bed for hours. The light from the burning man would flicker over our thighs.

Then there was a problem at work. Mr. Brune called me into his office and said that I didn't have a nose or an eye or an ear for news. He claimed that no part of my anatomy was suitable for the job. He said that I rambled, that my stories weren't accurate, that I seemed to invent news items. He said that I ignored the obvious and dwelled on the obscure. In my defense I said that I knew what readers wanted. And if a story didn't offer it, if it were too mundane, too ordinary, deficient in vitality or color, then what was the harm in a little embellishment? I wanted to say more, but Mr. Brune had the evidence on his side. "We're talking about life here," he said with an air of finality.

You probably won't believe this, but, as long as you've come this far, I want to tell you how my wife would turn into things. One night, shortly after I had been fired, we were sitting in the living room, and I looked up from my book and saw a window sitting in the chair where my wife had been. "Celeste," I called out, "where did the window come from?" Celeste reappeared in the chair. "I was thinking that I was a window," she said. It was then that we discovered my wife's talent for being anything she thought about. She could become a clay pot or a Tupperware bowl or a jar of jam. I always liked it best when she would turn into glass.

Jeremiah Stump, the stranger, said, "You might wonder why I've called you all together." My father was dying. No one could identify why, but there was no doubt about it. My sister dug up the flute and played the terrible music that my father called "Music for a Lady Sleeping in Japan." Though his face looked as if it had been sucked dry, he smiled thinly when he heard my sister playing. I left the room before the final moment. It was just as well. The Ma Yuan print hung on the living room wall. The lines faded and failed.

Once upon a time, a woman who desired and desired and desired more was lying in bed. She was not thinking of anything. She was not thinking of Nagasaki or Hiroshima and all the books that could have been read by that burning. She was not thinking of ships or the price of gold or the names of her lovers. The wind blew over her body. She could feel time flow back inside her.

My father's greatest disappearing act was performed at his funeral. It was not at all what I had expected; it was rather festive. The mayor was on hand and delivered a speech thanking my father for all the contributions he had made. Luckily, no one pressed him to give any examples. Someone asked the burning man if he would please move away from all the wreaths and flowers. "We don't want this to turn into a pyre." There was a curious light in my mother's face. It might have come from the glow of the burning man, but it also might have come from somewhere deep inside her. With her talent, my wife could have turned into anything: a wreath, a tear, a broken dish. I looked at her, and she knew what I was thinking. Right before everyone's eyes she turned into the sleeping lady of Japan.

As the years passed, my mother grew more serene, and it was disturbing to see a woman of so much vitality become lost in a grand vision of the design of things. Such tranquility! Such inner peace! We hated to disturb it. When the family would occasionally get together for Sunday meals, we would whisper. While she passed a plate of sliced ham or talked to us about the past, we'd see her see things that we could not see.

Still I wonder. And when I sleep, all the rain begins to fall on the Sleeping Lady of Japan. The children come and collect it in thimbles. Still I wonder. I wish that I had said something else to Mr. Brune. "This is not, Mr. Brune, in spite of all your good intentions, a believable world."

Patrick Lawler

MAPS

"Who was it who decided on where Tallahassee should be?" Toby asks questions, and we laugh a lot. Stupid things really. But it makes you think, and it helps to pass the time. He takes the money when people pump their gas, and I do most of the other things, like brake jobs, tires, and shocks. Mostly minor repairs, quick jobs that get a good price for the boss. Mr. Cutter keeps things under control and drives the tow truck when somebody breaks down on the highway. That's how he makes his big money. He says when you break down on the interstate, you become desperate. "The main thing we give them is a sense of security," says Mr. Cutter. I call him Mr. Cutter, but everybody else calls him Harry because the name of the business is Harry's Gas Station. "If we didn't charge 'em a lot, they'd think we did a half-assed job," he tells me and Toby. And later Toby says to me, "Using that logic, we should charge Harry a whole lot more for what we do." Toby mostly takes care of the cash register and points out the restrooms and gives people change for the cigarette machine. And he sells candy and soda to the sweaty little kids and tells the traveling salesmen where the phone is. And he hands out maps when the customers want them.

Maps

You can't say anything to Toby. He's always changing it around and making it funny. Mr. Cutter's always saying Toby's nothing but a smart-ass college kid. But I don't find anything wrong with having a little fun. Toby graduated from a community college and is going to a four-year. Though he's smarter in a lot of ways, I've been here sixteen years, and I know a lot more about cars. But, boy, Toby knows more about everything else. I could tell Betty kind of liked Toby, but I didn't pay much attention to it.

Like I said, Mr. Cutter owns the station, but he isn't around much because of driving the tow truck, and he owns another station, where the town people go for gas. I've worked for him for sixteen years. I know he doesn't like Betty coming around because he thinks she distracts me. We get a lot of business in the summer. There are always cars boiling over and people always need gas. Most of our customers come off the interstate. Toby started working after college let out for the summer. Mr. Cutter told him right away to call him Harry, but he never said that to me. We don't get many locals because we're a little overpriced. Toby lives up north, but he has an uncle who lives here so he asked Mr. Cutter for a job. And he started calling him Harry right away.

Just to make things more interesting, Toby decided that we should do something with the maps, so we uncreased them and laid them out on the desk in the office. People are always asking for maps because people are always going places. Toby told them not to trust those GPS things, and he told the customers, "There's nothing like a map to get you to where you're going." Toby took some scissors and began snapping them. When he was finished, there were a whole bunch of cities lying on top of the desk. Peoria, Orlando, Savannah, Nashville, Columbus. He told me to refold the maps and put them back in the racks. Toby said, "Think about it. A couple driving along, looking for Tallahassee. The husband turns to his wife and asks her to check the map. She pulls it out and says Tallahassee's not there. And he says, 'What do you mean, it's not there?' And she says, 'Look, there's a hole where Tallahassee should be.'" Toby has a real imagination. When we were finished, the desk looked like a battlefield with all these fallen cities. Every state had at least one city gone. So no matter where anybody was going there'd be something missing. At least, that's the way Toby saw it.

Betty and I have always known for the last three years we are going to be married. She works in the local diner as a waitress. We've been saving our money because we think by the beginning of next year we can afford a trailer. I'm ten years older than she is, but her parents like that. Mr. Dodd says that I'm a "maturing influence." I knew she kind of liked Toby because she'd laugh at things he'd say even if they weren't funny. That's one thing you learn about women. Most of the time Toby is funny, so I didn't much notice. Betty is twenty-two, which I think is a perfect age.

Toby decided that we weren't finished with the maps, so on another day he pulls out this little white bottle from the desk drawer. In the office we have an old Royal typewriter that keeps breaking down. Mr. Cutter says we got to get a computer, but he says that every time the typewriter's not working, and what he says doesn't amount to much when it comes to spending money. The typewriter has so much grease on the keys, you can't really make out any of the letters. And that's why I didn't know we had any Wite-Out and didn't know what it was. Toby found it. He likes to rummage through Mr. Cutter's stuff. I tell him he better be careful, but guys like Toby don't have to be as careful as guys like me. I found that out most of my life. So Toby takes the Wite-Out and asks me to get the maps off the rack. Then he begins dabbing the little white brush like he's painting with shoe polish. When he's finished, he takes a black pen from his shirt pocket and very carefully writes something. He has real small handwriting anyway—but this was ridiculously small and perfect. He dabbed away the word Tuscaloosa and wrote in Vacancy. "How do you like that?" he said, and he held up the map for me to see. "Vacancy, Alabama." He dabbed out Pearl, Mississippi, and wrote in Ruby. He replaced Hopkins Hollow, Connecticut, with Hopkins Hole. Sometimes he'd write in something that was a little off-color, like Beaver Shot, Oklahoma, or Pussy, Oregon, or Cock, Wisconsin. "Some old maid," he said, "will be asking directions for Cock. Or some minister will be seeking Pussy." I have to admit it was pretty funny.

We get all the license plates through here. At one time or another, I've seen the license plates of every single state, and that includes Hawaii and Alaska. I may not have been many places, I tell people, but a lot of places have been to see me. You got to see something after sixteen years. After I'd seen the license plates of all fifty states, I got to admit the job became kind of routine. I know Toby is young, even insensitive at times, but he makes the job enjoyable. He's always got something going on. And sometimes he gets me thinking, like when he asks me if I believe in something and I say yes, and he shows me I didn't really mean to say yes. That kind of thing. Then Toby has these crazy questions, like puzzles, that can keep you going crazy for days.

I have to tell you something else he thought of that was pretty good—though some might not understand. We had this little hole we drilled in the side of the ladies' restroom. We hid it behind boxes and oil cans. After we drilled, he had me chisel out some so we could see at a better angle. It made me feel a little uncomfortable, but Toby said, "Hey, there's no harm in just looking." I felt bad in a way and only pretended to look. Toby said that the New York State license had the best pair of legs he'd ever seen, and I agreed though I had no reason to.

Toby wasn't finished with the maps either. He got real tricky. Sometimes with green, red, and blue Magic Markers we'd put in other highways. Where we thought it might be nice to have a highway, we put it in. Without any inconvenience, without any cost, without any dusty detours, wham, we made you a highway. Just like that. We had an interstate going from Charlotte to Fayetteville to Lynchburg to Charleston to Knoxville. Some of our state highways climbed out of lakes and other times they'd drift off to nowhere. Sometimes we'd put roads where they seemed to be needed, and at times they were just useless and pretty. Some states seemed to have so many roads they didn't know what to do with them, but we'd add more until the whole map was choked with them.

We got so good at altering the maps that we moved some cities from one state to another. We'd put Spokane where New Bedford should be, and Little Rock where Spokane should be, and Topeka where Little Rock should be. I tell you we got good at it. Toby'd say, "We're doing the country a favor."

About two weeks ago, Toby came into work real upset, like I'd never seen him before. I don't know if he had an argument with Mr. Cutter or his uncle. But something was wrong, so I told him I'd take care of the pump if he'd work at fixing the air hose that seemed to be clogged. Betty came over during her break. She bought me some metric wrenches from the Ace Hardware. I told her she shouldn't have done it because we're trying to save money to buy a trailer and we're going to get married, probably in February. It was a sunny day and that made the oil stains next to the gas pumps sparkle in a greasy sort of way. Nothing's prettier than a gas station on a sunny day. It was a real scorcher. There was a haze around the car hoods. Betty said she had to get back to the restaurant, but she had to use the ladies' room first. I got her the keys which were attached to a flat piece of wood that said "restroom." I was about to take the lug nuts off a Ford truck when I thought about the peephole. I was hoping no cars would pull up because Toby was fixing the air hose and I was going to the back room. I pushed aside a couple of smudgy oil cans and pressed my eye to the hole. There was Betty with her back leaning on the wall over the sink, her dress up around her waist and Toby there. The weather and the cramped dark room made me feel real uncomfortable. I thought about the box of metric wrenches. Then a horn started to blow. Later, when I saw Betty, she handed me the key. Her eyes looked crushed. They had the color of one of those oil stains. Her body seemed to hum. Before she left, I thanked her for the wrenches.

Toby's going back north in a couple of days. I found out that Betty put a picture of herself in his glove compartment. I can't be mad at Betty. Toby is sure better looking, and he certainly is smarter and funnier. I say I saw the license plates of all fifty states, but that's not the truth. I don't think of buying the trailer anymore, but that will probably change. I decided not to say anything to her or Toby. Toby would only turn it around and get me laughing. And if I said anything to Betty, I'd feel really hollow inside. I went to Toby's car and opened up the glove compartment.

I don't laugh as much at Toby's jokes. He's always thinking up something new, but I don't pay as much attention. He asks me what is wrong, but I don't say much. "Nothing," I say and that's usually the end of it. In a way, I'm not looking forward to the day when Toby's gone. But I know one thing. I'll keep handing out our maps to the customers. I'll give them maps with a couple of things missing, a border here and there, a capital or two, a city or a town, some river misplaced. But they'll also contain some amazing new things. Highways that never before existed. New cities or old cities in new places. And wherever these people are going, they'll always be surprised at how we got them there, even if it's not where they want to be. Still, they'll always be surprised, and that's not so bad. They could wind up anywhere and that would be worth it, I suppose.

I'd kind of like to be there when Toby opens up the glove compartment. I know he'll see Betty's picture, and that will probably make him feel good. And then he'll see the road map, and I know he'll open it because he'll guess something is up. It took me a long time to do it, and he'll appreciate that. I'd like to see his face when he sees every town and highway and everything with its new name. "Betty" written everywhere. Betty mountains. Cities named Betty. Betty rivers. Betty highways. Who knows? Maybe his car will break down. And he won't know where to tell anybody where he is if something bad happens. It will make him feel kind of weird. Being so smart and all. Except about cars and things that can happen. He'll think somebody knows something. It won't really matter, but it will give him something to think about.

Patrick Lawler

SKYWRITING

The sky opened for the planes and closed up quietly behind them. The couple sat in the airport restaurant, looking at each other over the plastic redandwhite checked tablecloth. She was a singer for the revolutionaries. He was a skywriter who was running out of words.

For years they came to the airport restaurant owned by the Greeks, and they talked about Blake or shared Andrew Wyeth's Helga pictures or discussed the pre-Socratics. Under the sign that read "Daedalus Cafe," they shared poetry and revealed how they would make love to each other—if only things were different. The delicious details: under a sky full of stars, their bodies like weightless birds, touching each other the way an eyelid touches an eye, entering each other the way sound enters an ear. They wove fantasies together until they became more real than the lives they were living. She let him dwell in her past; he showed her the places he had fallen.

"All my men were miners and war pilots." At first he thought she said "mirrors." And he pictured beautiful men moving through her life with her face and her body.

Skywriting

"All my women were hagiologists and onion farmers." At first she thought he said "radiologists." And she saw him surrounded by glowing women who were on the verge of an incredible sorrow.

She watched his tiny plane totter in front of its exhalation of words. The letters piled into one another. The clouds were made from the skin of plums. The blond fields like mats below him, he skimmed the autumn-blood trees.

She said, "I dreamt you were touching another woman's hair."

Sometimes she became her past for him. In the airport cafe with the redandwhite checked tablecloths, she turned into a young girl singing in a church, opening her hymnal the way she opened her lips. Or she again was pregnant with her son, and pulled him from her womb so the man could see the child. Or she showed him the time when she was first touched by a boy, his tongue spiraling around in her ear. Or she breast-fed her son, having her body turn into light and food—the breast flowing with her first milk. No one in the airport noticed, though the Greek woman—short and dark and wise—often smiled. And on the murals Hephaestus skipped.

He pushed back one of her stray hairs. The sky over the airport was pale while they soaked in each other. She touched the hairs on his arm. They were like pieces of a puzzle that fit perfectly together. Pegasus took off and the togaed philosophers frolicked. The man and woman were the words written in each other's open book.

The woman allowed him to be part of her past so his memories were her memories. They talked about the secret connection of things—how they were really the same person living different lives.

He was enthusiastic with new facts. "Turgenev's brain weighed 4.7 pounds," he said.

"Is that a good thing?" she asked.

"It's remarkable when you realize an average brain weighs three pounds. If you think of it." He pressed his hands on the napkin as if it were a scale. "Of course, you have to take into consideration how much a thought weighs." Humus was puttied inside the pita.

"I think it's terrible. Brains should be light," she said. "They should be buoyant. They should be like . . ."

"Clouds?"

"Yes, that's it exactly. Like smoke but not really. Maybe more like a testicle." On the wall Socrates stood with his vial of hemlock. "Old Turgenev must have been stooped with the big rock of his head. He would never have understood my songs."

Out the big window they could see the skidandbump and bumpandskid of the landing airplanes.

She always knew there was a difference between her saying and her singing. Though she was paid to sing for everyone, she thought of herself as singing only for the revolutionaries, those who saw differently, those who knew they lived inside bodies, those on the verge of losing everything for the sake of a vision. She imagined only they truly understood the words. Men whose brains were like clouds; women whose brains were like smoke. She told him about the nineteenth-century essayist Hearn, who wrote about a cricket who ate both its legs before it died of hunger. "He said there are human crickets who must eat their own hearts in order to sing. I know exactly what he meant."

He watched her eat—nothing extravagant—a pizza or sandwich frilled with lettuce that the Greek woman made. He marveled at the movement of the woman's hands, the movement of her teeth. He wanted to be the food that touched her lips. He wanted to slide down her throat, to be digested, to turn into her cells. There were times, however, when she wouldn't eat. She would sit and watch the food.

"What's the matter?"

"Nothing." A woman in a toga walked away.

"We'll order something else."

She felt the tears inside the food—and she was afraid she would choke on it the same way as a little girl she had choked on the host. "Oh, go ahead," they would say. "It is only God."

"You are my baklava," he said, and she drenched his mouth with a sticky sweetness. He would have touched her breasts as if he were making bread. He would have memorized all the places on her hip. He would have had his whisper nestle in her ear. If only things were different.

The airport was designed for biplanes, small passenger planes, and crop dusters trailing sweet fluffy plumes. On the walls of the airport were columns with bluewhite clouds and women in whiteblue togas. The man and the woman were reminded of Keats's diorama of unrelieved hunger.

Other times she would eat everything and still be hungry. She wanted everything on her lips. She wanted the silvery juices of fruits; she wanted breast milk, its benevolence; she wanted song.

Because he had never seen her body, he relied on the descriptions she provided. With their mouths their words had sex. Words like wild berries. Like blood drops from a building that was melting inside them. She said her orgasm was her body breaking into song. She said it was her soul trying to get out.

They pretended to be waiting for someone from another country. "Portugal," he'd say. "Thailand," she'd answer. He looked up from his tuna fish sandwich into her rain forest eyes; the women in togas sparkled on the walls while the Greek gods seemed heavy. Most conversations revolved around previous conversations. They could endlessly listen to each other's words. They filled each other with them. He vowed to love her for all time. "Or at least until that guy arrives from Portugal," he'd say. And she'd respond, "Well, that will be a very long time—since he's coming in by way of Thailand."

She told him stories about her son, and the man felt as if she were telling him stories about his own past. She asked him to keep a journal. He would write to her music. She would tell him about the men in her life: the ruby miners in Cambodia, the coal miners in Virginia, the diamond miners in South Africa. She said, "That is why I am in love with women."

Dazed and airsick before they even stepped into the air, the travelers were groggy as their sensible garment bags were folded beside tables.

When she left for long periods of time, she would send him directions or maps or descriptions—anything that would bring him to her.

We counted seven deer asleep beside the highway.
The radio carried its map of noise—sad men read about the
weather behind us.
We passed dark, polluted water.
My heart is at the end of a key chain.
We needed a way to hold the songs together.
We brought our lives with us—as much of them as we could carry.
My boy read riddles as we passed through wine country.
What has a musical mind and lives in the sky?

Skywriting

All the while we moved the air in our car from one place to another.
I am connected as we drag everything behind us.
Love.

Once she brought him a kerchief with drops of her menstrual blood. "I want you to see this," she said. He took it in his hands as if he were preparing to study for a test. The red linen of her inner life. The ancient script. Sometimes she would give him articles of her clothing, and the next time they were together he would show her a picture of himself wearing whatever it was she had given him: a lemon scarf, some dark nylons, a pair of heels. The pictures made her smile.

He said, "I sometimes wake up and think I am inside your dream."

He always picked up the order of food and waited on her while she always paid. Thinking of his journey, he said, "I'm tired of living in the sky."

She said, "I'm tired of living in other men's minds."

"So how is the revolution coming along?" he asked.

"It feels like I'm trying to move stars," she said.

The outside moved in with the inside.

The Greek owners served falafel and pizza and calzones.

The waiters used the Socratic method.

They handed out an inductive menu.

He brought her his journal of sky scribblings: "My navel is a reminder that I come from you." His plane snored through the clouds.

Patrick Lawler

Letters spun out behind him. An alphabet of fur and smoke and future rain. His writing was lopsided.

He bumped across the clouds.

"I will never eat a bird," she said. "It would be like I were eating part of the sky." She remembered what God tasted like. She remembered the darkness in her mouth. The mural in the cafe pictured Eros with an arrow aimed into his own heart. She remembered how her son touched her breasts with the air that was inside his mouth.

A whole river flowed past their table. He asked her to describe what her fingers felt like. "It's like entering a cloud," she said. They had swallowed a thousand-year-old secret of each other and now they were on the verge of divulging it.

He announced, "Since 1939, the electromagnetic signals from every TV program ever broadcast have been hurtling toward the distant stars. They have arrived at over a thousand already. Lucy and Gilligan and Mr. Ed." They thought of the silent women in togas suffocating behind a layer of blue. This was after the Greek owners of the cafe had the mural painted over. Zeus and Aphrodite tried to look out from the thin skin of Mediterranean color. When he was in his airplane writing things in the sky, his words would not stand still. They were always on the verge of dissolving. He tried to complete what he had to say before the beginning of it was gone.

The airport was full of graffiti in different languages. They marveled at its power—the pure force of something mysterious and unstoppable. Something that is both known and unknowable. "Everything I do," she said, "is for my son." The painters rolled their rollers over the words.

Skywriting

They watched the sky travelers, tired, snapping at each other like poodles. Dragging luggage behind them, avoiding the stepladders, trying to evade security.

"Why don't you try the Zeno salad?" asked the waiter—but it never arrived.

The man sat in his flight jacket; she sat in an old silvery ball gown with an anarchist symbol shiny on the sleeve. They ate lobster bisque. "Do you know how they make love?" she said. "Who?" he asked. "Lobsters. It's after the female has molted, when her shell is still soft. When she is tender and vulnerable. That's when it happens."

One day after the woman returned from one of her trips, he told her he had kissed a hagiologist. He could barely see the blue-robed women in the murals. "Was there glowing?" she asked. "Can I ever forget?" she asked. "Did you open your mouth?" she asked. And he answered the only way he could.

She felt herself vanishing inside her own throat. He knew she needed time.

"I'm running out of worlds," she said.

He told her the only words that were real were the ones they said to each other, and already they were traveling past a thousand stars.

She said, "I am not a cricket. I will not eat my song." He had heard her sing only once. He was the revolutionary in the crowd in the Greek pizzeria in the tiny airport. He knew at that moment that he would always love her. Every time he went into the sky, he thought of her. His words flowed behind him, soft and billowy. White scoops of words. He turned everything in his world into her insides. What had he been thinking? He felt he would die in the celestial crawl space behind the clouds.

Patrick Lawler

That night, when she looked up at the sky, she saw him there, writing their conversations. It was a celebration, their words traveling past the thousand stars. It was a confession and an apology. The whole sky was alive with their dialogue. The night was blackandblack. The words were white and soft. The sliver of runway looked impossibly narrow.

And she began to sing the words she saw unfolding in the night. They both knew it was her voice which kept him from falling through the dark scraps of sky. The words she had given him kept him up in the air. Because her songs had other skies to fill, she knew that she would have to allow him to fall. His falling was his way to get back to her, so he fell through the words they had not yet spoken. He fell through the blue drying over the women in togas and the Greek gods. He fell through the air of her singing. And he fell.

Whenever she sang and wherever she sang, his falling was all around her.

Patrick Lawler

THE YEAR 1958 WAS LOST

1.

We thought it was natural for our grandmother to see things that were not there, just as it is natural for an astronomer to see into the darkness and pick out a star or for a microbiologist to see into the nothingness he puts on his slide or for an historian to see into the blue emptiness of the past and pick out a single moment.

2.

It was the year of the big snow and the year my grandmother wouldn't die. It was the year when 1958 was irrevocably lost. My grandmother came to live with us because she wasn't "quite right." Her skin grew to be the color of a broom. Every morning her heart kicked on, surprising all of us.

The Year 1958 Was Lost

3.

Matt, my brother, moved into my room while his room was altered. Wire glasses, a clock in the stomach of a gold horse, a gray water glass, teeth in a cereal bowl, murky pill bottles, stubby black shoes. And pictures, boxes of them, walls of them.

Our grandmother was detachable. We never dared look inside her black pocketbook with the silver-sounding click.

4.

My father taught history at the local high school. Matt and I did not want to get to tenth grade because we thought we might have him as a teacher. Unlike other fathers, our father would never come home and inform us about what he did during the day. After he surveyed the symmetry of the dining room table, after he stretched a napkin on his lap, after he cleared his throat with an *auugh,* he would tell us what happened in 1812 or 1916 or 1498.

5.

At the dinner table my grandmother said with an air of certainty, "In spite of what we hear, life is easy."

"She's slipping off her mind," my father mumbled under his breath.

"Don't listen to that nonsense," cautioned my mother.

6.

When my brother and I returned home from school, we'd sit on the edge of our grandmother's bed, her box of photos between us. The muddy photographs with the false and rigid poses passed from my hands to my brother's hands, then to my grandmother's and back again. "Okay, write on the back: 'Aunt Minnie.' No. 'Cousin Jim.'"

"What about the date?"

"1934. Yes, why not 1934?"

This business of identifying photographs was done, my grandmother said, to make her past "livable." My mother didn't like any of this, and my father only tolerated it because my grandmother was not *his* mother. He would say this with some relief, as if all responsibility for her behavior rested with my mother.

7.

At the time there were many mysteries.

Some of the mysteries included:

a. The man with the lean, chipped face.

b. The hole where a man had been.

c. The man who was trying to put his heart back inside.

8.

There were some questions about what was happening to my grandmother's mind. My mother insisted that there was a problem. "She's losing the past." My mother pleaded with my father to be more understanding. "Don't you see what's happening? She's losing one year at a time. Pretty soon there'll be only the present. And then . . ."

9.

"Who is this?" asked Matt.

"That's your grandfather," our grandmother said while she looked vacantly at the lean, chipped face. Later our mother said, "What are you saying? That is not *my* father."

10.

Because it was snowing, my grandmother was always calling me to the window. Matt was shoveling now. "Look," she said, and the snow flew back into his face from the shovel.

At night the light from the snowplow jumped into the curtains.

11.

My mother said to my father, "It isn't right. She looks at those damn pictures—she's got the boys doing it, too—and she makes things up."

"She's old," said my father, repeating what my mother had often said. "What harm can any of this do?"

"But she's lying. She's changing her life. She's reinventing her past."

"Maybe she's the one who's got it right," my father said. "We just can't stop inventing the past. It never ends. If we stopped for a moment, the whole thing would collapse." He wanted to say something and he lowered his voice. "History is just the present pulled backward."

My mother shook her head. "Thank you, Mister History Teacher, but I don't care what you say. It isn't right. That's not my father."

12.

My mother measured how far my grandmother had regressed by asking her questions while brushing out her hair.

"Well, I think it's happened," she announced to my father. "She's lost 1958."

13.

Quietly we looked at the picture of the man with the lean, chipped face. Our grandmother spoke, "When your grandfather died, it was as if he had gone out mowing, as if he'd walked out the door with every intention of coming back. It didn't really seem final. But when I cut up his shorts to use as dust rags, that's when I knew he would not return, and if he did, he would not be pleased. Since I did not want him back that way, I decided to live my life without him."

14.

Matt asked our father if it was easier to live or easier to remember.

Our father said, "Be quiet."

15.

Many of the pictures were cut up. Matt and I looked at the holes where faces once were. We looked quizzically at our grandmother. Her thin, white, flyaway hair. Her lumpy, blue legs.

The Year 1958 Was Lost

16.

I was in school, learning the names of rivers, when my grandmother got her stroke. The Missouri flowed, rushed by in a white rumble, while part of my grandmother stopped.

Everyone was called to the house. The kitchen was filled with floppy coats and black, shiny boots.

My brother assured me, "She's not going to die. Believe me, nobody dies with people all around them."

17.

Matt was only half-right. Her left half sagged.

A part of her was someplace else.

Her skin was wadded up; her bottom lip crumpled; her breath smelled like rotting pears.

18.

Nearly all of the photographs were put away. There was a picture of a man with his heart on the outside.

Her bedroom smelled bitter.

It was winter and the days grew smaller. The snow plopped up around the bushes. Dawn came out of the snow and not out of the sky.

The man with the heart was trying to put it back on the inside.

19.

"People will always try to tell you what life is like. Don't listen to them." She looked for her pictures under her bed. "Life is a twisted cloth tugged through a tiny hole." She opened up her pocketbook. "That's what people mean when they talk about time." She looked inside.

"But as the cloth comes out the other side of the hole, it becomes nothing. Now I'm on the other side of the hole." She clicked her pocketbook shut around the word "hole." "Now, let your mother know I want the pictures."

20.

Matt said he wanted to see the pictures, too, but our mother said she couldn't find them. My grandmother stared at her shoes. Matt didn't like to see her vacant eyes.

We sat on the side of her bed and he'd create pictures for her to see.

"Remember the one with the greenish film of dust. Remember the one with the waltzing couple. Remember the one with the gray humming man."

Our grandmother's belly grumbled like an old boiler.

"Remember the picture of a woman unpacking a cello. Remember the picture with the fountain and the swan."

21.

Matt was right about our grandmother not dying. Her feet would go *pat pat* in her dirty yellow slippers. And sometimes we would hear the tinkle of broken glass as things slipped through her fingers. Eventually my mother gave my grandmother photographs, and she went back to inking in names and dates and cutting out faces. She kept seeing things that were not there, like the day she saw Uncle Biff, who had been dead for five years, staring at her window from the snow. And dates still dropped out of her. She remembered nothing of 1958.

It was the year of the big snow and the year my grandmother wouldn't die. It was a year of mysteries: the man who was trying to put his heart back inside.

Matt asked our mother about some of the things he didn't understand.

And I asked our father.

We tried not to ask them again.

Patrick Lawler

THE LIFE AND LIFE OF WALTER OATS

I. The Concealed Pronoun

Walter hadn't made plans for being immortal. I sympathize with what some call his financial oversight and others claim to be his spiritual flaw, but, though moral lassitude can be blamed, I prefer to point a finger at an inactive imagination. His life is not so much an exercise in obstinacy as it is a parody of it. Walter lacks the energy and creativity to deviate from what comes so naturally: one breath and then another. I must admit that all of Walter's life, as immense as it may be, as trivial as it probably was, as far-fetched as some would believe, is really only rickety speculation. Still, it's that uncertainty which makes it teeter on the edge of the poetic. Walter, who I contend has no imagination, is there only to stimulate the creative impulse of others. Contrary to his effect upon me, I believe his life was normal. He submitted, I assume, unremittingly to the routine. Even his suffering, I imagine, was irrelevant. Hemorrhoids. Migraines. Allergies. A general irritability. Irregularity. In the face of all that was regular, of all that obeyed time and season and ceremony, he must have felt out of place, baffled, stranded in the bottomless hole he called himself. No matter how much I find it necessary to assume the extraordinary, I believe that no one detail, no one event was unique in his life. The only unusual thing about Walter is that Walter, for no apparent reason, lives forever.

I discovered him in room 302 in the west wing of Saint Erasmus. No matter how inventive I wish to be, I cannot escape from beginning in this rudimentary fashion. Time, place, person, muse. Pedestrian as it may be, it seems necessary. Time and sequence control me in a manner that they could never assume in the life of Walter Oats. Immortality, I have come to learn, has as one of its defining characteristics the fact that it releases one from the necessity to invent story. And so from the start, my narrative is limited—dare I say, flawed. Restricted by time, it must be entirely, unabashedly false. Nevertheless, I was admitted to Saint Erasmus for an emergency appendectomy. "I am a sick man," I said as I entered the emergency room, certain that all but perhaps my wife, who knew my inclination for inserting obscure allusions into everyday conversation, had missed my reference to the opening sentence of Dostoevsky's Underground Man. I must admit, however, the events leading up to the operation are blurred. Pain sharpened my senses but sharpened them inward, so that I was more aware of myself, but less aware of my surroundings. I remember chatter. Static. Nurses and orderlies had no faces; they scurried about and then vanished. Doctors were condescendingly absent while my wife was irritatingly present. After the operation and a brief period in the recovery room, I was transported to room 302.

The first two days were fogged by drugs. It was like reading a newspaper that's been cut up. Everything lacked continuity. Things would get interesting, and all of a sudden I wouldn't be there. On the third day I resumed one of my normal activities: thinking. I was still being treated to glucose and water and I was still drowsy and aching, but for an hour on that third day I picked through some of my notes on Tolstoy that my eldest son had managed to deliver. During the summer I had been gathering material for an article on Tolstoy which I hoped would be published. I called it "The Concealed Pronoun: The Inexplicable Itness behind the Curtains of Ivan Ilyich." As an Associate Professor in the English Department at Wade, I was expected to publish occasional spurts of scholarly acumen kindled by large doses of ego and opportunism. I didn't accomplish anything that third day. I only wanted to touch ground again, to relocate the objects of my life, to see if they still felt the same. I was like a man who lives in a bombed village who wakes everyone to make certain no one has disturbed the pieces of rubble he still wants to call home. My pieces were still there. Albert Drake, the Chair of my departmental "ant-heap," paradoxically diffident in manner and rumpled in attire, arrived with a pile of books. My wife, always the bearer of the banal, stopped by briefly with some news about a member of the department who was having an affair. Nurses starchily huddled behind curtains. My papers and books on Tolstoy scattered on the bed before me, doctors shuffled and mumbled and coughed.

Sometime during that day, between the changing of an IV bottle and some scribbled, uninspired notes on Tolstoy, I noticed that the bed beside me, half-hidden by a sickly green curtain, was occupied by an older man. Before, there was a lump, a blur, an indistinguishable hump of white sheets. That this represented a man I was certainly aware, but that this man was worthy of my attention, even a fraction of my distracted inquiry, never occurred to me. But now I required something else to occupy my mind. I had had enough of the hospital staff, my wife, Albert Drake—poor tedious Albert Drake—even Tolstoy. Here was a new diversion, a new dimension. There was something about this man—maybe an enigmatic look, a hint of a discriminating demeanor—that instilled in me a kind of curiosity. I felt as if I were studying the painting of a man and not a real man. Perhaps Bellini's *Doge Leonardo*—thin and elongated and focused, his hat like an elaborately painted urinal. Though his body was stiffened and his two- or three-day-old beard was jagged and gray, his face appeared placid, even serene. He blended into the sheets, white running into white. The head was buoyant on the pillow. What idea kept it afloat?

I later asked a nurse on the second shift (although the nurses on the second shift were less efficient, they were always more cordial) what this man was "in" for. I suspected she missed my attempt at humor.

She shrugged. "Let's roll on your side." I remained silent, waiting for her response.

"Does he have anything serious?" (Perhaps I was implying "contagious.") "Do they suspect that he'll die . . . I mean, in the near future?" (I was fearing the rude effrontery of a cart call late at night.) I felt the stiff sting of a needle. This man's death was a prospect I didn't welcome. I was an adamant believer that a stranger's death should be conducted in private. Even nature has animals sneak off into the woods so they don't flaunt the luridness of their dying.

"OK, that should help you sleep. You can turn over." She puttered around with her paraphernalia. "You mean Walter?" she asked when she was finished. "Well, to tell you the truth, we don't know that much about him. His name is Walter Oats. Poor man, really. It doesn't appear as if he is going to die."

I thought this was a curious comment from a nurse—either a weak attempt at humor (and I did find most of the staff to be humorless) or an expression of her exasperation over a lack of bed space (which I thought the more likely—though I didn't detect the slightest scent of irony in her voice). However, I did firmly believe she couldn't have meant that he was *never* expected to die. Luckily, I fell asleep before I could pursue this question, but in the morning it burst in on me at breakfast. I was irritated that the nurse the evening before had left everything out. She hadn't qualified her statement with an adverb or an adverbial phrase: *It doesn't appear as if he is going to die tomorrow . . . or going to die soon . . . or going to die for some time.* My irritation grew as I discovered a student I had taught in Freshman Comp. Student Nurse Evans, according to her name tag, was to be my nurse for the afternoon. Two points demand some clarification. First, I endured composition courses only because we were required, by an unsatisfactory compromise reached by the Head of our department with the Dean, to teach one a semester. As tedious and predictably unimaginative as the typical literature student can be, the composition students are dreadfully lacking not only in the rudimentary communication skills we so prematurely assign to our species but even in the most basic social skills. Second, I found it appalling that my care was turned over to a neophyte—though she explained that my regular nurse was supervising every aspect of my care. Wonderful, I thought. Two incompetent people for the exorbitant price of one. (Thank Zeus for two things: my insurance and my patience—one of which was far more reliable than the other.)

Nevertheless, my Student Nurse Evans, in an earnest manner, filled my water container. There was something in the way she maneuvered herself that made me recall *La Source* by Ingres—the elegant, nubile body lugging a vessel of liquid. Though I didn't recall Nurse Evans, she still remembered the class. I suspected she was one of those dull, uninspiring students who, try as they may, never have one worthwhile thought, one spark of an idea, and never even attain mediocrity. One of the many pretty faces to disguise the dreariness of the mind. A polished trinket in a world of trinkets. As always, this was my problem: I appeared to be the only one who saw the irony. Still, she provided me with the best opportunity to find out some answers about this Walter Oats—if only to complete the sentence uttered by the nurse on the second shift. After the aforementioned student nurse arrived to remove the tray that contained my lunch, a medley of synthetic-looking cuisine that remained embedded in plastic pools, I questioned her about my roommate.

"What is his diagnosis?" I asked bluntly.

"Not hungry, I see," she said as she reached for my tray with its jell-o or pudding—and its numerous colorful inedible globs. "It's good to see you're talkative," she added. Sometimes I felt I were lecturing in a room full of somnambulating sophomores sleepwalking in the chambers of academia and life. "Who knows?" she said. Keys dangled from her fingers as she picked up the tray. "Supposedly, he came here years and years ago, after a fire in a rest home forced the patients to be reassigned. I guess records were lost. Though his records here would fill a room."

"But you ignore him," I said, recalling that I had never seen a nurse attending him. His food trays sat untouched before him. His pillowcase had a grayish tint to it. As I questioned her, I also wondered at the grade I had given her. If she was to be taking care of me throughout the day, maybe I could suggest a retroactive grade change—as a motivation of sorts.

"And it hasn't affected his metabolism, his respiration. Frankly, all he does is breathe. And regardless of how many times we change his sheets or bathe him or roll him over or check his blood pressure, he does that quite well without us." The ectoplasm on the food tray trembled as she walked. After slipping the tray into a waiting cart just outside my door, she slid the keys into her white pocket. I thought of something I quite frequently said to colleagues in the presence of a comely coed: she's as pretty as a lecture.

Her curious response to my questions only made me more determined "to pluck out the heart" of Walter's mystery. For the next several days I questioned everyone who came in contact with me about the nature of Walter's illness—though I did become more careful about separating the distance between what I actually thought and what came out of my mouth. The nurse who passed out medications said, "Some believe he once existed with the aid of machines and before that with the assistance of home remedies and before that with magic and dancers." Magic and dancers, I thought. Surely now we've entered the realm of Student Nurse Evans's medical expertise. One of the doctors, a particularly remote woman, said in a blandly unconvincing tone, "In your condition, you shouldn't focus on such things. Try to get better." I inquired about Walter Oats's family, about his past, about any information I deemed relevant. I questioned nurses and doctors and religious people and social workers and hospital staff, anyone who would listen. Some would be passing by my door, and I would call them in for a chat, though I really received no reliable information. Walter breathed an average amount of air and limited himself to certain spontaneous movements, a jerk of a leg or a flop of an arm. The nurses kept tabs on what entered him and what left him. Blood pressure and temperature were methodically recorded until Walter's life dwindled into the details. Whole volumes were kept on him, though huge chunks of time were missing: months and years had vanished, the original diagnosis long forgotten. Sometimes the nurses neglected him for weeks, but then as if inspired, they'd suddenly resume the records and tirelessly pursue Walter through the figures on the charts until once again, due to apathy or malaise, they'd forget that he was even there or hoped that if they stayed away, he'd either shrink or vanish. But Walter wasn't going anywhere; he just wouldn't budge.

There were so many versions of his life. One of the oldest nurses claimed to have met Walter's wife. According to the nurse, the relatives started complaining. It just took Walter so long to die that they simply lost interest. Others still asked the wife about Walter, so she had to adopt a word to describe his condition, a verb to connect him to the living. "Lingers." Daily she ran through her conjugation. Oh, Walter lingers. Oh, Walter lingers nicely. Oh, Walter lingers not so well. But then, according to the older nurse, it took so long that people simply forgot to ask the wife about her husband. A little while more, and she forgot the answers.

A male nurse who worked the third shift said that the older nurse was lying. "She hasn't been right for years," said the young man.

One of the doctors (I called him Dr. Bianchon) confirmed this, saying that it was pure fabrication and that everything I would hear about Walter would be unreliable. "Some of us have invented Walter," he said with sad authority. "We see in him whatever we want. We aren't even certain if Walter is his real name." The doctor was puffy and thoroughly disagreeable, which gave him an air of credibility, and I noted his odd obsession with psychiatry. I decided to be blunt. I asked him how long he thought Walter could live. Dr. Bianchon pondered, crunched up an eyebrow, and said, "He *could* last forever."

I remained in the hospital for five days, and during that time I never encountered one individual who could refute the claim that perhaps Walter was not going to die. The evidence seemed to suggest that in Saint Erasmus Hospital in room 302 there lived a man who was going to keep living in spite of the neglect, in spite of the rumors, and in spite of the odds against it. The prospect was exhilarating. After I had packed my bags with socks and underwear and pajamas and stuffed my books and papers in a grocery bag provided by my wife, I went over to Walter's bed. It was the closest I had been to him. I placed my hand on his hand and said something trite that would have been, under normal conditions, an effrontery to my sense of propriety and taste. "I'm sure we will meet again. I'm sure of that." Never before in life did I feel such joy. Upon reflection, I know this seems an odd admission, but consider the hopefulness this man offered. I was ready to explode. By the time the wheelchair arrived, I was feeling my Oats, so to speak.

Student Nurse Evans rolled me away down the hall to my wife's open car door—and from the chair to the car I wobbled helplessly back to the quotidian.

II. Research

Upon returning home, I was greeted with the cool indifference to which I had become accustomed. My home life was a situation tragedy. I have three children: a Jungian, a Freudian, and one who passionately, obstinately believes in nothing. My young Raskolnikov. They were characteristically miserable, icy replicas of real people. And then there was my wife. Our relationship lacked even malevolence, and that really hurt. Our marriage had grown impoverished, pallid. Jonathan Edwards would have approved of our sex life—and I'm pretty certain which of us would have been the "loathsome spider." Our bedroom could just as well have been a mausoleum. Except for the iridescent dial of the clock that kept telling me I was awake, nothing was alive in that room. In this semistygian atmosphere, you would think my enthusiasm for Walter would have diminished, but it didn't. I was obsessed.

I confronted my wife with the situation and my interpretation of it. "Don't you view it as a distinct possibility? For once in your life, use your imagination. Doesn't it in any way excite you?" She continued reading her book on postmodern theory. "Damn it," I uncharacteristically shouted.

"Why do you persist in this foolishness?" Her head lifted out of the book and her eyes adjusted to reading my face. "What about your article, your classes, your . . . your family? You seem to be slipping back. That's all I'm saying." She positioned herself behind a neat row of words.

Surprisingly, I experienced little discomfort from my incision. In fact, it was healing so rapidly, I could barely determine where it had once been. Nevertheless, I decided to take a sabbatical. Though it was rather late in the year to apply for the leave, I had not taken one since coming to Wade, and, with my past scholarship, my convalescence, my alleged project on

Patrick Lawler

Tolstoy, I had very little difficulty in having my proposal accepted. But I had decided to hell with Tolstoy, with Ivan Ilyich, and to the relief of scholars everywhere, my essay would never get written. Instead, I needed the time to piece things together, not only for myself, but for Walter. Because he didn't have a satisfactory life, I assumed it was my responsibility to invent one. So while my wife and daughter and two sons slept, I worked deep into the night—diligent and determined.

My insomnia was a blessing, a hermitage, a cocoon, where I could escape from my family's cluttered lives through my own distracted life and into Walter's pure and empty life. Between one and four in the morning, time exists only for the pursuit of timelessness. To my great relief, I could pursue his life instead of my own. Between one and four in the morning, I conducted my dialogue with the clock, and therein lies the paradox. Hadn't Walter climbed out of the box of time? Hadn't he left it behind? Flabby time. Disconcerting time. Crinkled time. Between these serpentine hours of one and four in the morning, I began to compile what I viewed was a profile of an immortal, based on the evidence I had gathered on Walter Oats.

I had all these urgent questions that needed to be answered, but there wasn't any place to begin. There wasn't anyone who could remember Walter's life, how it differed from a neighbor's, how it rattled when it was cold, how it snapped with fear or jiggled with laughter, how it banged or gulped or bellowed. If Walter remembered, he kept it locked inside. Was he really married, and how many times? What were his occupations? His education? Did he prefer a beaujolais or a chablis? Did he read Tolstoy or Dostoevsky? Balzac or Pushkin? Had he ever been to Greece? I installed his past, imagined his future. His mapmaker, I gave him continents, flattened some areas, fattened others, but I never gave him boundaries. I wrote and wrote until Walter existed more completely, more vividly in my notebooks than he ever could in room 302.

All these urgent questions needed to be answered. Between my morning inoculation of coffee and the deepest part of the night, I tried to fashion a life for Walter.

Every question I pursued spilled into other questions. My notebooks bulged with possibilities. What is the sex life of an immortal? What would heat the glue of passion? Wasn't time, after all, measured and always moving, an essential ingredient of the sensual? One would quickly tire of Keats's urn. Didn't the prospect of death add an air of urgency and maybe even dignity to the whole proceeding we call life—grabbing hold of the flesh while the flesh is still there?

Maybe a little too much carpe diem—or maybe just too much carping.

What did he mutter when he stubbed a toe?

What made him sad?

What was his diet?

What were his dreams?

Were there any religious connotations here? I hoped not.

I marveled at all the seismological repercussions—all of literature would have to be rewritten, all philosophy would have to be rethought, all religion would have to be scribbled out and reenvisioned.

Preparing him for his odyssey, I invented characters: a Circe-like temptress with an insatiable spirituality (there would be moments when they would lie in bed, emptying into each other's arms); a Penelope waiting, waiting with subdued carnality, always waiting, dependable, predictable, waiting. And in the end a priest who is slain and a poet who is saved. But, of course, that was the problem: there was no end. As soon as I gave Walter a life, I had to invent another. Each mythic quest piled on top of all the others. An epic in futility: a marriage that didn't work, Walter's sowing of his surname, dissatisfaction, escape, return, escape, children who despised him through their obedience, useless gestures, compromises, and finally his transcendence and immersion rolled into one. Again the word "finally" undermined the very nature of Walter. Sometimes I made him a horologist, skilled in the measurements of time; sometimes I made him a poet, timed in the measurements of skill. After some research, I discovered that Saint Erasmus is the patron saint of bowel disorders. Was this a clue or another diversion? My scholarly inclinations took over as I collected quotes almost in a compulsive manner. Where would a scholar be without the appropriate quote to add resonance to an observation, to add heft to an argument? I found them everywhere—in books, on my shelves, on my desk. It seemed that nearly everything I had ever read led me to Walter.

If it be dreadful to die peradventure it is more perilous to live long: blissful is he that hath the hour of his death ever before his eyes and that every day disposeth himself to die.

Thomas à Kempis had a point. There is something unreliable, sinister perhaps, about a man who doesn't die.

Nevertheless, like Balzac, I labored. I kept exact track of every imagined event of Walter's life—the whole immense chronology, methodically indicating what was on his mind and what was in his pocket.

The Life and Life of Walter Oats

But there was a nagging concern. Walter was perhaps only a beautiful device to divert me from what was essential and painfully obvious: my own life, my own exiguous life, and ultimately *my own death*. And then sometimes I entertained the thought that his insistence upon breathing, this dismissive attitude toward propriety, was opposed to the very idea of life, in that it stole from life any meaning and in turn denied it any destination. I had to consider some possible explanations:

a) Time was Walter's occupation.

b) Death has to be earned, and Walter, through some oversight on his part, hadn't earned it.

c) Walter was simply more durable than most—so enough with the metaphysical prattle.

d) Walter didn't know he was supposed to die. (And at a certain point—from lassitude or apathy—no one was willing to tell him.)

He defied my devotion to symmetry, and the notebooks began to accumulate with my attempt to discover the shape of Walter's life. My theses were formidable. I created a colossal universe through which Walter could stumble, and the questions were overwhelming. Did he know the difference between an Ionic column and a Doric column? Did he ever have hypertension? Did he know the names and locations of the constellations? Had he ever tasted sleep on the cheek of a woman? Had he been to Westminster Abbey? Had he read *The Brothers Karamazov*? Did he appreciate Bach? With his name singing of the earth, golden and substantial, Walter went on and on and on.

III. Unfinished

My life resumed, and I eventually lost my enthusiasm for Walter Oats. He was no more than a passing phase—something akin to my adolescent regard for Dylan Thomas.

My daughter, the Jungian, had been married and was teaching. My older son, the Freudian, was pursuing his Ph.D. in another city, in another discipline, and might as well have been in another universe. And my younger son, the nihilist, decided life wasn't worth it—went off, returned, and went off again. Perhaps I should digress to characterize the "home front." My current wife had been a former student and now was a junior colleague who was on the verge of receiving tenure. My three children are from my first marriage, to a dutiful, unimaginative woman, who, I claimed in a self-congratulatory tone at a department gathering, resided in the "trailer park of the intellect." Though I never said so, and would deny it if pressed, my current wife resided in the postmodern amusement park of the brain, where things zip along and twirl and eventually everything ends up upside down. We couldn't have a civilized conversation that didn't include her refrains of sarcastic comments in protest of what she claimed was my sarcastic tone. What she once referred to at a department party as my "sweet cynicism" became a target of her passive-aggressiveness, her insipid jabs, her carefully constructed barbs. She dismissed me with the comment, "How can you say that, with all that has been going on? I stood by you and now you come up with this." I wasn't entirely certain what the "this" referred to. Her fatal error was believing that she was my intellectual equal. This was the condition. We didn't inhabit a battlefield any longer; rather, we resided in the banality and suspicions of a neutralized zone where an occasional potshot ricochets from a guard station, but mostly there was a miasma of silence and wariness, with the terrible expectation that everything would burst through. We barely look at each other across the bleak landscape of foggy bridges and barbed wire and border booths we'd constructed in our bedroom. I noted with some agitation during her affair with Albert Drake that the further she removed herself from me, the happier she was. And so I reluctantly took up my various roles as teacher, husband, father—all unsatisfactory efforts to compartmentalize me.

Through the years, there grew a heightened sense of my own mortality as I'd hear the grind of bone on bone, feel the nip at my insides, hear the enervated thump of the heart. In short, I became loaded down with my life, its routines, its obligations, its own controlled hysteria. I seemed to roll over in place like the gear of a clock. I was "wearied out with the contraries," to use a phrase by Wordsworth. Lacking any curiosity about my own life, I lost the authority to meaningfully give it any contours. I had blown it up with each breath, given it its numerous coherent recognizable shapes, but I went further and every breath after that point gave it a new monstrous body until it was an indecipherable lump—heavy, contorted. Nevertheless, I was trapped by it—no matter how hideous. If I let go of it, the impact of the escaping air, the sudden and startling exhalation of all I had put into it, would topple me over into a pile of bones.

Such was my condition when my wife was scheduled to have a hysterectomy at Saint Erasmus. I had forgotten the character of the place, the Dantesque landscape. I suspected Cerberus would poke one of his three heads around a corner. I remembered, when I returned to the hospital, the trash bags puffed with tissue, cotton balls, and gauze. I remembered the terrible tiled rooms and the insidious machinery that seemed to have been rescued from a distant inquisition. After my wife was admitted, I thought of Walter Oats. Once again I had to relocate my pieces. I went to room 302. A nurse, Ms. Evans, older now, less perky, even somewhat sour, was bountifully bent over a patient. "Where's Walter?" I asked.

"I'm sorry?" she said, turning in my direction.

"Walter Oats."

"Walter Oats? Yes. Walter Oats," she said, returning to the patient. "He's no longer with us." Something shook loose inside me. Walter, I must admit, hadn't had any influence on me for years; nevertheless, I suspected he survived as a secret source of inspiration. I suppose I believed he wasn't really immortal, but still I must have held onto the possibility, and somewhere inside me I must have nurtured it while it nurtured me. During a very difficult period, my recovery, in a very real sense, had relied on the hope that Walter began to represent. I didn't want to say the word dead, but I did.

"Oh, no." Ms. Evans turned to me again and seemed to recognize me. In her predictably inarticulate manner, she informed me that she hadn't meant that Mr. Oats was dead, only that he had been moved to another floor. "Actually, Walter has improved. I'll take you to him if you let me finish here." My favorite grade to issue a student was an incomplete. I issued it with relish, knowing that the student would never finish the work that was expected, and after frustration and guilt the I would turn into an F without any inconvenience or commitment on my part. I was certain that is what Ms. Evans received from me. And in his own way, that's what Walter was receiving.

She explained on the way to the fourth floor that Walter was more alert. "He's more in touch with reality," she said cryptically. We passed the nurses' station. "He sits up now. He is less afraid. He doesn't really speak to anyone, but he is much better. At least he doesn't have to stay on that floor." When we arrived in the day room, she pointed to a high-backed chair and said, "I'd better get going now." I thanked her and walked toward Walter.

I could have parodied Ivan Ilyich; I could have said, "Well, he's alive but I'm dead!" But that would have been a sorry exaggeration.

I had forgotten how Walter looked. In my abstractions, in my endless reflections between one and four in the morning, in my own sparkling blue notebooks, I had lost the reality that was Walter, the shriveled body that was Walter, the three-day-old gray beard that was Walter. His eyes were glazed with the shellac of distraction. There was a vinegary smell that lingered about his body. Was this the man I had given Penelope to? He sat, staring out the window, his eyes stuck to a tree or an auto or a brick in a building. The sky was a weighty gray color. It seemed to enter the room. Each of his pupils were puttied in place.

I longed for some kind of affirmation, some kind of epiphanic revelation to spill over the moment: the color fell out of his eyes. I longed for some kind of reassuring statement: his foot tapped to a terrible prehistoric rhythm. I needed an illumination, a glaring, sudden flash: there was only the fleet and feeble light expiring beyond the window. I required his triumph, and he withheld it from me. Was there any rage left, any fierce intensity? Was this what they called "getting better"?

The irony. I had once entered the hospital to have something removed from my belly so I wouldn't die, only to have something like hope installed in my head. Now it seemed harder to determine what was more poisonous.

Patrick Lawler

There he sat, draining away. All the pasts I'd given him—the everlasting future, too—it didn't seem to matter. Those thin and fragile fingers. Those bony legs. Had I overestimated his talent for survival? What is it that hides from us the things we most ought to know? What pain or what veil or what insipid sense of pride? It started to drizzle and the window glass blistered with tiny raindrops. When I turned to leave, I felt his blood slowly paddle its way through his veins. Everyone seemed to believe that life was the illusion concealing the great abyss of death. But suppose it were reversed? Then it struck me. Walter was not over. No. What had perished were my efforts to fashion for him a life. What perished was the Walter that existed in my notebooks, the Walter that assumed those grotesque shapes in my mind. The real Walter wasn't finished. He sat, looking at the rain fall, without any deviation from what came so naturally, from what came so beautifully: one breath and then another.

Patrick Lawler

WAKE US AND WE DROWN

1.

"There are some things in nature that just don't belong there," my father
said as he carried her upstairs and lowered her on the bed in the guest
room. My father slumped in his baggy fishing coat; my mother in her
yellow housecoat stiffened like a pencil. The sickish light from the lamp fell
into the mermaid's hair, thick and gummed and greenish. The light lay on
her shoulder like seaweed. I think my mother said she smelled like a violin
rotting in the rain. Back then nothing was predictable: words jumped out
of nowhere. "Let her sleep," my father said.

All the next day, after my mother gave her a sponge bath, the
mermaid lounged on the couch. Immune to the grayish blur of the TV,
she looked at us bewildered, smothered, her dreamy, vacant eyes like
putty. I don't remember anyone speaking all afternoon. A terrible stillness
revolved around the mermaid's body while the TV muttered in low, dull
vowels. I had to see what she had seen. But that's the way things were. Fish:
thin, silvery, tarnished; fat ones like blue slippers; black, floppy ones like

rain rubbers; tinny ones that floated past the Sunday paper folded up on a chair.

My mother did not hum that day. Her patience, her reticence, instilled in me a kind of courage. I don't know what she fed the mermaid, but whatever it was turned into sleep.

2.

That Monday, before my father went to work, he carried the mermaid down to the living room and arranged her on the couch. Propped with pillows, she lay with her fin dipped off the cushion, like the wing of an exhausted bird.

I went to school but never told anyone what my father had found. I sat at my desk and watched the blackboard eraser sweep across the board, taking with it the Civil War—more thorough than Sherman. Atlanta was buried in a cloud of chalk dust, and Southern ladies with hair that fell in wide curls, ladies with huge fans and yellow voile, sat on big white porches. Back and forth—the fan, the rocker—the fan wiping out a green hill, the smell of jonquils, a Southern gentleman's face. The fan sweeping back, the hill and flowers reappearing. But not the face.

That's when I learned the capacity that things have for being there and the greater capacity for them to be wiped out. Chancellorsville. Vicksburg. Gettysburg. The *Monitor*. The *Merrimac*. Dates would rise and fall:

April 12, 1860
September 17, 1862
April 9, 1865
May 20, 1961

Time collapsed into white dust.

3.

When my father returned home from work that evening, he carried some boxes under his arms. "Swimsuits," he announced. And he asked my mother to alter them.

"What for?" my mother asked.

"That's the least I can do. Don't you think I feel responsible?"

After we ate, my father asked my mother to knit a pillow in the shape of a shell. "Who do you think I am? Lloyd Bridges with a needle?"

"At least you can help make her feel at home," my father said.

"I don't think that's my job," said my mother definitively.

I cut construction paper into finned, fat shapes. Later I suspended the grape and orange and cadmium fish from strings over the mermaid's bed. I put in the eyes, huge, black dots, with a Magic Marker, and it dried up before I finished so that some of the fish were blind, drifting lazily from their strings.

My father painted the room. He rolled out strips of chilly blue sky. "It's the color of water," he corrected, as melancholy dotted his hands and sleeves.

We worked all that week. When we were finished, my father stepped into the doorway. Proud. Isolated. Spots of sky on his hands and trousers. "The pillow would have been a nice touch," he said to my mother. Knowing that there would be no reply, he never asked the mermaid what she thought of the room. I think my mother mumbled something about the piano we could not afford.

I suspected all my father's efforts would only sabotage his plans and actually work in reverse. I imagined the mermaid drifting in a huge, thick nostalgia for the sea.

It was near the end of school, and I sat at my desk, diagramming sentences. The textbook. The carved-out letters on the desktop. Words piled up. Back then nothing was predictable.

I   revolved

fish   nothingness

4.

"What next?" asked my mother. "Do you intend to flood her room? And if that doesn't work, flood the house?"

So my father decided an in-ground pool would be appropriate. And while the mermaid sliced through the blue waters of the pool, my mother folded laundry between working part-time at the hospital gift shop and taking an evening class in poetry at the community college. She went on observing the silent rituals associated with an ordinary life, though they seemed to have less and less significance in the presence of a mermaid. Worry began to appear in the movements of my mother's hands every time she imagined the piano my father said we could not afford. The routines began to lose their ability to order the day, to fill it with meaning, purpose, resolve.

"I don't think we should be raising a son in this kind of atmosphere," said my mother. "It doesn't seem appropriate. What kind of message are we sending?"

Because we could not afford a piano, my father gave my mother music books as gifts at Christmas, her birthday, Mother's Day. Opening these books lifted my mother into another world, the dots on the musical notes floating like the lost eyes of the fish that had no eyes because the black Magic Marker had dried up.

My father said we needed to make some changes, nothing too big. "For example, I don't think it's suitable to announce we are going to eat at a seafood restaurant. That doesn't mean we can't—but I don't think we should say it. That's all."

My mother was not pleased. "You are carrying this thing too far," she said. "It's not like any of us are ordering mermaid, for godsake. Though maybe some of us wish we could."

And whenever I asked my father about the circumstances of his finding the mermaid, whenever I'd approach him with why she had to stay, he always responded the same way. "There are some things in nature that just don't belong there."

5.

At night, the mermaid, smelling slightly of chlorine, would stretch on the diving board with the solid stars overhead, with the liquid stars below. Then eventually my father would come to pick her up and carry her into the house. Puddles of water formed on the carpet from the aluminum flash of her fin.

My father would carry her up the stairs while my mother read her music books, sometimes humming. While the rest of the house remained relatively unchanged, conservative with its dim, dull respectability, just above us a bedroom shimmered in an erotic blue, paper fish swam in circles, and a mermaid dreamed of the sweetness of the sea.

One day in the middle of summer vacation, the house was empty. The mermaid sat in a lounge chair by the side of the pool. I passed the guest room door and for no apparent reason decided to go inside. I came across the mermaid's bathing suits like puddles of jell-o: strawberry, orange, lime.

After getting scissors out of the hall closet, I cut the bathing suits into slices of exotic fruit.

That evening my father discovered the swimsuits but didn't get mad. He stood solemn and slumped; the order he had tried to establish was crumbling. I looked into his eyes. They had fallen into something icy.

6.

During that entire summer, we had a fear of unexpected guests, especially after the incident with Uncle Ralph.

And suddenly I found myself drawn to the mermaid, the enigma of her origins, the mystery of her hair, the mystery of her eyes. Late in the summer I entered her room while she was sleeping. The whole space was alert to the tiniest breezes, to an opening door, to a draft through a window. One could not breathe without causing the room to vibrate.

Her hips were plush and spongy. Her bottom half looked metallic like the color of an old watch, and yet it appeared to be soft, a petal, an ash. I put one hand on her breast.

Do not wake up now.

No.

Not now.

A warm slushiness shifted inside me. A lightlessness erased my brain. I saw what she had seen—the inside of something gigantic and teeming with life. Something immense and intimate at the same time. A place where all distinctions were blurred.

I remembered that after the incident with Uncle Ralph, because the mermaid couldn't sleep, my mother read one of the poems that had been assigned in her poetry class. The next day my mother, my father, and me were sitting at the red, faded picnic table. My father said Uncle Ralph was not to return to the house. I didn't mind because I never liked Uncle Ralph, his wobbly stomach, the cloud of cigar smoke that drifted through the living room and up the stairs.

7.

"I can't figure it out," said my father after the mermaid became sick. "I checked the chemicals in the pool. Everything seems perfect. The water. Her food. Her room."

The mermaid's eyes resembled the eyes of the paper fish. Big and blank.

My mother said, "Something has got to be done."

"What do you want from me? I mean, I can't drag her off to an emergency room. 'I'm sorry, sir, but we don't take care of things with fins. Maybe you should try a vet.' What do you want me to do?"

As the summer began to loosen, the mermaid became sicker. My father no longer brought her to the pool. She made movements with her lips but nothing came out. My mother said she smelled like a cello that had been sunk inside an aquarium.

My mother brought her a gift from the hospital gift shop: a clock in a seashell. "I don't know if time means much to her, but I thought the seashell would be nice."

"It is," I said.

8.

One day we woke up and the mermaid was gone.

It was surprising that none of us really asked any questions. It was almost like we didn't want to know. It was as if the mermaid had never lived with us.

In the fall I returned to school, where I again would have to sort through what had vanished and what would return—when I again would have to reenter wars that would have to be lost in order to be understood. And again words would pile up; words would jump off the ledges created in the diagrams.

The windup shell-clock eventually stopped, and time kept going away. The dark cover closed over the pool like a lid and the TV came back on.

My mother returned with a fervor to reading her music books, but this time they were spread out in front of the piano she bought for herself. She discovered she wasn't musically gifted, but she loved sitting there. She still hummed, but her humming was more beautiful.

Uncle Ralph remarried, but we weren't invited to the wedding.

My father painted the mermaid's room black and cut out the eyes of the fish that had eyes; the others he left alone, and they shivered as if someone were breathing when the door was finally closed.

Patrick Lawler

WHEN THE TREES SPEAK

There is no way I could handle the cutting, the dragging, the stacking. And to suggest my sister would be involved is certainly absurd. She's got more on her mind. And why would I arrange the logs in a self-incriminating way? I personally feel that would be ridiculous. Why would I leave my name at the scene of the crime—if that's what you want to call it? None of it makes much sense, but especially that part.

Should I speak louder or anything? I mean, is this thing on? I don't want to have to do this again. OK, I guess this is my statement. That's it, right? First, let me say I didn't do it. And second, I don't know who did. That should be the end of it—but I know how people talk, so I just want to set the record straight. Though you should know this: I wouldn't be upset if the person never got caught. Nothing against you, Ike. I mean, I know you got a job to do—protecting people and like that. But I got my job, too. Not as important in some ways, but in some other ways it's even more important. Helping to put a roof over people's heads is nothing to look down at.

When the Trees Speak

Of course, everybody has to realize I got more respect for property than your average person. That's got to be apparent. Anybody who doesn't see that has to have a head examination. And I was as surprised as anybody could be when I saw what that Sam Thrash had written on the trees, but I was even more surprised later. He said he didn't know who vandalized his property, but he still blamed me for bringing around people like that.

They were a good couple. Not be-backs.

You know. We'll "be back" with you after we talk it over. We'll check with our parents about the down payment, and we'll "be back." Of course, you hear that enough and you know what they're really saying. But they weren't like that. They were making a serious inquiry about the house, and I know they were interested. Of course, not after what Thrash did.

I like the feel of an empty house. I guess you got to in my business. I spend more time in empty houses than in houses that have furniture. That seems a little weird if you think about it. Still, the emptiness always surprises me. The gray fuzz along the floorboards. The little immaculate rectangles where pictures had been hung. The indentations in the carpet. The trick, if you want to sell someone one of these houses, is you got to have them see their whole lives fitting inside all that emptiness. Which brings me to the Simmons couple.

I'm not naive—or crazy. I knew people wouldn't be happy. Hey, remember my family has a history in this town, too. So I know how people can be upset when you sell a house to someone who is different.

And I know what people are thinking. There's no reason to bring my sister into this. Who she married is her own business. Angie hasn't been around for years, and just because she comes back, people start pointing fingers. So, I bring the Simmons couple to the old Comstock place. Too bad they're dead, and too bad their kids don't have enough respect for them to keep the house in the family. But that's just the way people are these days. No respect for property. I got to admit the house isn't much, but I wasn't about to say that to someone who was looking at buying it. One of those old farmhouses that inside are claustrophobic in a comfortable sort of way—small rooms with drafty spaces and old wooden, shaky windows. You try not to mention the utility bills if you can help it. So it was the second time I was showing the house, and I was complimenting the property and the view from the kitchen window. The kitchen is a calm green color. I'll bet you didn't know that in the early part of the twentieth century, it was determined that the color apple green had a calming effect, so police stations and insane asylums were painted green. And here's what interests me—husbands painted kitchens green. Just a little history. Maybe that's why I never got married.

Anyway, I was opening up the curtains on the kitchen windows so I could impress the Simmons with the scenery. Pastures. Woods. Stone fences. A row of pretty white birch. And when we looked out, we saw that word staring at us from the trees. Each white birch tree with a big black painted letter. And the word NIGGER staring right at us from the edge of the woods when I opened the curtains.

And what was I supposed to say, "Welcome to the neighborhood, Mr. and Mrs. Simmons. You'll get along real fine"?

Of course, it had to be that Thrash. As you know yourself. And when I confronted him, he says it's freedom of speech because the trees are on his property and they're just letters. "And if you see things there," he said, "then that's because you shouldn't bring people around who are

When the Trees Speak

sensitive to words." I was so mad, as you know. And maybe if you had done something back then, then nothing else would have happened.

Is that thing still recording? 'Cause this is the important part. Since my name seems to be a part of this investigation—if that's what you want to call it—then let me tell you something. My mother wanted to be Ginger Rogers—not that I really remember. So naming me Ginger was just my mother's way of giving me her dancing, but, of course, things like that don't work out. My mother'd say, "You're my little dancer." And she'd hold my hands over my head and move me like a marionette. But it would hurt my arms and shoulders the way she'd twist me into a spin. I think she gave me the dancing part of herself to protect it from my father. But I felt I needed to be protected from my mother. Not from anything intentionally bad—only her love.

Anyway, when my sister named her baby after me, that was just about one of the most important things that could happen in my life.

Of course, our father thought it was some kind of sacrilege. But anything that had to do with Angie and Miles was ugly, according to my father. And certainly a kid—no matter what you called it—was the worst thing ever. Actually, when Ginger died in her crib, some of my sister died, too. And because my mother had recently passed away, Angie wanted her daughter to be buried here. That's when our father said there'd be a blizzard in hades before he'd let that happen.

I always say you can't live your life inside something without having it take on your smell. You can't bump around without leaving some dents. The Comstocks' skin cells are still in their carpets. People try not to think about it—but it's a fact. My mother in a very real way still tries

80

to dance in our home—the one Angie says I should move out of now that Mom is dead and our father is in the nursing home.

Given what happens to each of us, I never understood why people hate other people just because of their color. Hey, the way I look at it is everybody's money is green and everybody's blood is red.

The best time to sell a house is in the spring as long as the basements aren't flooded. Things just look better when they're coming back to life. I like showing start-up homes to young couples when the whole long groan of their lives lies ahead of them. From marriage to kids to emptiness to age, our homes endure us. Ike, you know how some people can read palms or knotty skulls. I can read houses. Just by walking in them, I get a sense of the lives that have been lived inside their walls. And it's not a comfortable feeling.

When Angie first told our father about Miles, my father looked like he was passing a kidney stone as big a brick. He used to say that there was a clause in the Constitution that allowed the slaveholding states to count each slave as three-fifths of a person for purposes of representation. "The worst thing we ever done," he said, "is add the two-fifths." When Angie told our father about the marriage, he took a gun and just placed it on the kitchen table and said she better get away from him before somebody found himself dead.

Then, as you know, Angie left and got her education. And I was proud of her. It meant there was the possibility of leaving and doing something. Not that getting a real estate license doesn't involve learning. I'm not sure what she graduated in, but I do know she's trying to start up the landscape business since she moved back to town.

As I said, they named the child after me—which was an honor. But then she died unexpectedly, and they eventually separated. When a child dies, they say you lose a leg on a table. You still have the table but it keeps falling over. You do what you can to keep it up. But no matter what you do, it's always about to topple over. My father said some mean things, but the worst was when he said that Angie could never bury her kid in this town. "We don't need any evidence that it ever existed. There'll never be anything in this town for anybody to remember who doesn't already know what color that kid was—as long as I'm alive," he said.

After our mother died from that stroke and Angie was gone and I was trying to do what I could to take care of my father, he said to me one night he was going to tell me about my name. And I said I already knew the Ginger Rogers story, and he said it wasn't true. My father said my mother took ginger for her morning sickness when she was pregnant with me. That's what gave her the idea, according to him. What kind of legacy is that? I was named after something to stop vomiting. Angie said that at least it's better than being named after something that causes vomiting. I said, "Like what?" And she said, "Like our father."

That's another reason they never got along. They both speak their minds.

There's a thin line between saying the truth and not saying the truth. There was this house down by the old toxic dump—the Darby place. It had your usual scars to commemorate lives being lived—measuring marks scratched into the door molding. Things like that. But it had something else, a shoulder-high black stain from this gooey stuff that would ooze into the basement each spring. And this customer asked me if I knew what it was and if it was dangerous. And after I said I didn't know and I didn't think it was dangerous, the fellow said he was going to buy the house because I was being honest. That was over ten years ago, and his wife has cancer now, but we know it's just coincidence. It's just regular cancer, not one of those exotic kinds that could be connected to something toxic. If you are honest with people, it is always the best. And part of being honest is not saying too much—so you don't have to go to the place where you might actually have to say something that isn't the truth. There's a fine line between pointing out the problems and taking delight in the problems. I used to say that to Angie when she'd be in one of her arguments with our father.

Houses are a lot like people. All the changes. The transformations. I guess the point is to have the interiors and exteriors blend seamlessly. I know when I go to the place where they sell For Sale signs, they have a *For Sale Signs For Sale* sign in front of the place.

You know Angie came back to help me with making a decision about our father. The doctor said he was about 60 percent in terms of his heart and lungs, but the real problem was his brain. He'd forget things. Not just memories but things you need to know to stay alive. When you found him wandering, well, I knew something had to be done, but I needed Angie to say it for me. I saw how wounded she was. And then she tries to appear strong by analyzing other people. That way, she doesn't have to admit her own pain.

Angie said she thought I was pathetic. "A woman trying to sell her past," she said. "Every house is the home of your childhood," she said.

I said, "OK, Dr. Fraud."

My sister has led a life full of exclamation marks; I've lived a life full of commas. Nothing ends, nothing begins, nothing changes. I sell change—but I don't live it. I can't leave the house I was born in. When I was a child I always felt I was in danger of being devoured. I don't know where that came from. But now I know it was the house that was swallowing me. But there's always the possibility someplace else will be worse. So maybe Angie is right. I keep selling the house—but never have to leave. I just watch everybody else's life change around me.

Sometimes the houses look OK from the outside, but things inside aren't right—even dangerous, with aluminum wiring ready to spark, with inferior plumbing leaking under the sinks, with water ready to burst into the basement each spring, with plywood rotting under the roof. Things can look OK from the outside. That's my point. Is it worth taking the risk?

Maybe the Comstock kids are right. We grieve too much for our houses. Maybe it's just better to walk away.

Even in my own house I sometimes go into my living room and see my mother propped with pillows, sitting there after her stroke made her flop to one side.

I'm off the subject a little, but all I know is the Simmons couple were standing in the green kitchen, and I admit I felt bad when I opened that curtain, not just because I was losing a sale and not just because of what happened to my sister. I think I felt bad because of me. Because I never stood up for my sister when she got married. Not even when she tried to have her baby buried next to our mother.

But you got to believe this. My sister wouldn't just cut down trees. She respects nature. I know you say they were infected, but I wonder if my sister would have known that. How could she—or either of us—chop them up in one-foot sections so the letters were preserved and then arranged to spell out something different—stacked in front of old Sam Thrash's house, the word GINGER right there in his front yard for everyone to see.

I don't think I'm the kind of person who could be that obvious. I wouldn't leave behind my signature. I got to believe it was coincidence.

Do you have to change the tape or anything? I've been going on, I know. I'm like you, Ike, in a lot of ways. My job means I have to know people. It surprises me how some open up inside like a paper fan and you see the full pattern—some trees, a stream, a house. Or at least there should be a house with a For Sale sign in the front. Then I know other people who close up like a fist. And there's nothing but a darkness the size of a walnut—impenetrable and tough. When Angie came back, it was like she was trying to find that fourth leg for the table. Trying to keep things from tipping over. I said she could move in with me, but she said she didn't know how I did it. There were all the memories and most of them not great. You know I sold her that house across from you. Some houses are just too pretty to ever live inside. And I wonder what our father would say about her coming back. Angie says it's hard for him to speak his mind now when he doesn't really have one.

I told Angie I would do whatever it took to get her whole again. I used my trick when I showed her the house. I had her imagine her whole life fitting inside it. All the bare rooms full of potential.

I never told anybody this, Ike, but I guess that's what this is for, some kind of confession. You know, near the end, when I could still take care of my mother, I'd prop her in the chair. She couldn't really talk, and she couldn't really move. Somehow I knew what she wanted. And you know me, Ike, a bit big and a bit clumsy, but I danced for her. With my invisible Fred Astaire, I spun around. And my mother's big, empty eyes filled up with all the things that had been taken away from her.

When the Trees Speak

So anyway, if you think me or Angie had anything to do with chopping down Sam Thrash's trees, well, you better get an appointment because you need a head examination.

Yeah, my father's doing all right—considering. Angie just saw him yesterday. She said he looked afraid. She said we're all afraid—just of different things, but mostly of each other. I guess he was particularly irritable. She said she had something to tell him, and he was not happy. I asked her what color his room was, but she said she didn't notice. She said, "I'll be back." And I had to laugh a little.

RADIO

I knew how to make my father's life a living hell. I'd talk to him. I'd say, "Hi." And he'd say, "Can't you see I'm busy?" Then he'd lower the magnifying visor over his eyes.

Every day my mother looked like someone different. "I can't believe Mom is doing this to us," Abbey said. Abbey is my older sister, and I said, "They're just wigs."

In many ways our town lived in our basement. Things appeared to be one thing when they were really something else. That's what I learned listening to all those radios—not even trying to listen to them really—but the scratchy voices seeping up through the floor anyway.

Mike, my younger brother, was afraid of the woods behind the house—where he said he heard the noise of something awful waking up. Abbey said it was probably a nocturnal predator. In retrospect, I suppose it could have been an expression of a primitive longing—maybe terrible and musical at the same time, if by "musical" you mean the sound that comes out of something in deep pain. Seriously, I suspected it was just the noises from the radios, but no one ever listens to me.

Abbey was taking an astronomy class. She was studying the planets. "I can't believe a planet named after the goddess of love would have rocks so hot they glow. Sounds more like hell." She liked her teacher, Mr. Blunkett.

I heard my mother talking to my father about Mike. "He's being tested for sensory integration dysfunction and autistic spectrum disorder." My father slunk down to the basement, where his radios lived.

He was building a ham radio. I asked him once why they called it ham, and he said, "Can't you see I'm busy?" And then the cat flicked its tail, and my father yelled, "Get Moses out of here. Kevin, do you hear me?" He always asked me that. What was I supposed to say, "No"?

All of our animals—the hamster, the cat, and the fish—were named after biblical characters. My father said, "I don't care if we aren't religious. At least, we can have respect."

My mother had different names for her wigs—and they all began with S. Samantha. Sabrina. Sally. Sarah. Suzanne.

"Stupid," said Abbey. "I'm just saying that one of them should be named Stupid. I don't believe she is doing this."

I had to admit the radio my father was building was beautiful. It was a perfect city on the printed circuit board, with electric streets and tiny inns with fascinating names like "toroids" and "crystals," "resisters" and "capacitors," with intriguing shapes like monolithic pillow shapes and electrolytic can shapes.

In the woods my brother heard an ancient sleeping. Animals lurched in the darkness. Mike wasn't what you would call normal. And

I'm not being mean. It's just a fact. But no one would say that around me or they'd find their face in a world of hurt.

In school I was always being called to the office. They'd talk to me and I'd do homework and other things. Writing stuff and drawing stuff. The problem is once you get a reputation, they always blame you for things.

Voices lived in our basement—pieces here and there that represented lives. Along with the ham radio he was building, my father had a police scanner that picked up fires and crimes and accidents. He had another scanner tuned to the closest airport. His Probe 2004 picked up cell phones and cordless phones. The voices hummed and crackled.

On top of our mother's bedroom dresser were Styrofoam heads where her fake hair ripened. Zachariah moved through the openings in the plastic castle in the fish tank.

I never told anyone—not even my sister—but when no one was around, I would go down in the basement and look over my father's work on his radio. I checked off different steps as if he'd done them. Sometimes I'd go down in the cellar with my mother's nail polish and change the colors on the tiny parts. Of course, this messed up everything, but my father never figured it out. His calibrations were always off, but he didn't have a clue.

Everybody complained that my father was always working on his radio. I complained, too. But in reality I didn't mind that he stayed in the cellar. In fact, my intention was to keep him there.

The Styrofoam heads in my mother's bedroom carried on their conversations.

Radio

Sabrina jauntily came into the living room. Her hair bounced like a wheat field. "Don't be naive," Abbey said. "Can't you see what's going on? I shouldn't even be talking to you about this. For chrissake, can't you figure it out? Mom is having an affair."

Moses lived his life as a motor curled up in a corner of the basement.

My father had soldered something that resembled a tiny Ferris wheel in the middle of his circuit board. It was like a miniature version of the wheel in Nebuchadnezzar's cage. The basement was a swirl of sounds. We pressed our ears to the town walls. Worlds rolled over each other. The fire chief, the librarian, Mike's grammar school teacher—all had their secrets and indiscretions. Mayor Cheever and the proper Wescotts. Abortions and addictions. Affairs and "tendencies." People dying. People quarreling. People stealing from each other. Voices came out of their holes. My father's scanners were picking up accusations about Mr. Blunkett, Abbey's astronomy teacher.

When people made fun of Mike, I'd have to threaten to beat somebody up, which—to admit it—meant that Abbey would have to get involved since I really wasn't much good at fighting, though I have to say I didn't mind getting beat up in defense of my brother.

It was as if our mother was hidden behind the wigs. Sally's hair was the color of a lemon. Sarah's hair was like a freckle—pinkish-brown. Sylvia's hair was as black as a tire patch. "Look at her," Abbey said.

"I just think the wigs make her feel good. It doesn't mean she's having an affair," I said.

"Look at her life," said Abbey. "Why else would she be happy?"

I went down in the basement and wrote on one of my father's diagrams.

I heard my mother talking to my father. "He's being tested for pervasive developmental disorder and Asperger's syndrome." What upset me was that Mike had no idea. If they felt there was something wrong with him, why didn't they just talk to him? I wanted to tell him not to be afraid—but I also felt it was too late.

The Styrofoam heads slept with their eyes open.

"Does it have anything to do with eggs?" I asked my father. And he looked strange.

I'm still not sure what happened. I think about it, but I don't know if I was too young and I've mixed up what my sister says with what my father says. For some reason, it's important right now to get my version of the story straight.

Underneath our mother's tide of dark hair, it was as if she were trying to remember herself. I expected the stars to come out of her hair. I asked Abbey if what they were saying about Mr. Blunkett was true, and she said she didn't think so. "But you never know," she said.

Nebuchadnezzar whirled around in his silver cage. The heads on my mother's dresser hung around like tourists.

My sister says I'm wrong about most of this. She says she never knew anything about Venus. She says she never said anything about how love and hell are so close together they can smell each other. All I know is I wouldn't make something like that up.

I do know that she said, "If Mom does die . . ."

"What are you talking about?" I asked.

"I probably shouldn't be saying anything. Mom's not having an affair," said Abbey.

"That's good," I said.

"Not really," she said. And she laid the pamphlet for wigs on my bed.

"Jesus," I said. I read the words on the front. JUST BECAUSE YOU ARE UNDERGOING CHEMOTHERAPY DOESN'T MEAN YOU CAN'T LOOK PRETTY.

I couldn't keep Mike from being afraid of the woods. He'd stand at the window of his bedroom. If you went deep enough into the woods, he was convinced there was a brightening. I told him that wasn't a bad thing, and he said it was. I said, "Mike, don't listen to what people say." His eyes were like pellets.

The basement was where my father prayed. He sat at the helm of his basement worktable, soldering toy buildings to a miniature city. And all around him was the undertow of voices and indiscretions dragging him down. I suppose what he really prayed for was for the rest of us to vanish so he could be alone with his voices. "My life is a living hell," he mumbled.

My father stormed out of the cellar, flapping around a piece of paper with my writing on it. "This is it," he screamed. "I can't take it. And Mike? What is this supposed to mean?"

I heard my mother and father talking in the tone of voice they always used when they were talking about Mike. "ADHD. Bipolar. What happened to just plain weird?" asked my father. "No more testing. Kevin's just gonna have to get by without a label."

"Maybe he just has an overactive imagination," said my mother.

Looking at Mike's eyes, I could tell his heart was in a world of hurt. "I saw him go into the woods," said Mike. "It was as if he were closing a door behind him."

"Who?" I asked.

"Mr. Blunkett."

"I think I know why Mom got all those wigs," said Abbey. "When it happens, we won't really know who it is that dies. Samantha or Sally or one of them will die—but Mom will still be here. It's perfect, really."

"My life is a living Venus," I said. And my father didn't know what to say.

My mother said to Abbey, "Protect yourself."

In the fish tank, Isaac swam like crazy, as if he were trying to get away from the water. Mike stood at his bedroom window, looking out toward the woods. My father was lost in the depth of his miniature city. The voices moved as if they had long ago left us behind.

My mother called me into the room where the white heads slept in their clouds. She took my face in her hands and brought me to the fire of her wig. "It's OK," said my mother. "Talk to me."

Patrick Lawler

MY FATHER'S SUICIDE NOTE

After my father started writing his suicide note, I gave him a thesaurus. He never took anything lightly, and I knew he would approach this task with the same commitment to clarity and preciseness that he put into everything else. Given his attention to detail, I knew the thesaurus would help to delay things.

Because people in the town were outraged by the subject of the course, Mr. Higley, the teacher in our Health and Human Sexuality class, agreed to avoid any references to human sex. Instead, he provided us with examples from the animal kingdom. He wrote on the blackboard: *The smallest penis on Earth is a fraction of a thousandth of an inch.* "That should make Todd feel pretty secure," said Nykole. Once Todd had shown us his penis just before math. I can't say I knew what to expect. But I will say it wasn't something you needed to look at twice. It was more interesting than decimals but nowhere near as intriguing as my grandmother's name.

Elizabeth Hart. I thought it was the most beautiful name I would ever hear. After my father's father had died, my grandmother took her maiden name. "Why shouldn't I live the last years of my life with the name of my mother?" Some people in the town viewed her with suspicion because she was always advocating for a cause. She vigorously protested what she found to be unfair and just plain wrong. Once she ran for political office on the issue that the chemical company should clean up its toxic site. There was still a smattering of signs with my grandmother's faded picture on people's lawns. VOTE FOR CHANGE, the yard signs read. "This town wears its Hart on its lawns," Sheriff Wilby said. "But it's not like change is a good thing," he added, shaking his head. And my grandmother was doing fine until she was picked up for shoplifting.

When the cheerleaders waited for the school bus, their skin looked like caramel. The rising sun was strangled in the power lines. Nykole, my best friend, twirled her hair until it sounded like music. Her skin was sugary.

I made other efforts at prolonging my father's suicide attempt. "I'm not sure what that means," I'd say. "Maybe a footnote would help." Or I'd suggest that he include a glossary. He agreed with me. "There's no sense in confusing people. I should be as clear about things as I possibly can."

I decided to show Todd my breasts once I had them—but Nykole said once I did, I'd change my mind. "Before you have them, it's easy to think of them as not belonging to you. But once they're there . . . Well, things are different." While Nykole brushed tangles out of my hair, Todd told us his parents were getting a divorce.

My Uncle Bob, in an aluminum lawn chair with the webbing unraveling until he was held up only with faded blue whiskers, sat in front of the sweet corn stand. Though there wasn't any corn, cars would still stop and ask how Uncle Bob was doing or about my grandmother. "What happened to the corn?" they'd ask, and he'd point to the house with my grandmother in it. "She blames the power lines, but you know she's crazy. She says one of the first things the Puritans did was steal the corn from the Indians. She's not right. In the head. That's why I stay here. Or else I'd be someplace else."

When I told my mother, she said, "Don't listen to him, Keira. If anybody knows what crazy is, it is Uncle Bob. Not from watching someone else, but from his own personal experience." The dead deer, their antlers busted through their skulls like calcified fountains, looked out from Uncle Bob's TV.

Nykole told me that she was digging a tunnel out of her house. Todd's stomach made a noise. It waited at the end of everything. Electricity clung to the air above the town. Knots of it. Nykole and I said we would be sisters forever.

After my grandmother was picked up for shoplifting, she explained that everything is connected. "My hands grow around these things. It's like these items are returning to me. Over a distance." The owner of the grocery store explained to my mother that he had allowed my grandmother to shoplift for years, and he had finally had enough. "Times are tough," he said and called in Jake Wilby, the town sheriff. "Hold it right there," Jake said to my grandmother as the pack of gum slid into her purse.

In our Health and Human Sexuality class our teacher passed out a handout: *Female chimpanzees are astonishingly promiscuous. Some have been recorded copulating with eight different males in 15 minutes.* "They must be cheerleaders," said Nykole, while Todd looked longingly at their breasts. The part where his chin became his throat resembled the belly of a frog.

My Father's Suicide Note

My mother spent nights reading my father's insurance policy, determined to find the loopholes. "Maybe you could consider doing it incrementally," my mother said to my father. "Removing a body part at a time. I think it would make more sense. They pay pretty good for limb amputation. I'm not suggesting you should make an occupation of your demise. But there are practical considerations."

My uncle, his face like a dart, said he hated people who started things and didn't finish them. "I'm not saying anything—or anything," he said when my mother looked at him disapprovingly. He was carrying his rifle over his shoulder. "Going target shooting by the waste beds," he said. "'Be like a bullet' is my philosophy. You start off in one direction. You can't all of a sudden change it. You got to see things to their completion. That's all I'm saying."

I remember that when there was corn, me and my grandmother would husk it on the back porch, and she would talk about the way the sun, the dirt, the rain were enticed into being these gold nuggets.

"That's what I mean," said Uncle Bob.

For our history project each of the students was given a prison that we were supposed to recreate. Todd had Buchenwald. Nykole had Attica. I had Andersonville. Nykole said she felt sorry for the cheerleaders—their skinniness, their expectations, their shiny smiles. The way they called out cheers at football games as if their words of encouragement mattered. As if they had an impact. The letter *W* for "Warners HS" curved over their breasts. Todd looked longingly as the cheerleaders constructed the tiger cages of Con Son Island. Mr. Actaeon, the history teacher, said, "I don't think they had night lights in the tiger cages." And the cheerleaders rolled their numerous eyes.

Most of what Uncle Bob said started with the words "those people." "Those people don't know what they're talking about." "Those people gotta learn a thing or two." Or sometimes he'd say, "That's just the way those people are."

With her face all crinkled, my grandmother explained the absence of corn. She said the power lines which Uncle Bob had permitted to go up on her property were affecting everything.

"The only thing it affected," said Uncle Bob, "is our wallets, which got bigger—and her mind, which got smaller."

My grandmother said, "What happens with the power lines is they create a current. They make something not happen in one place, and take that and make it happen someplace else. It's not natural."

"She stopped taking her pills," said Uncle Bob.

When we learned that one testicle of the average blue whale can weigh up to a hundred pounds, Todd looked uncomfortable. When Todd asked questions in class, the cheerleaders lifted their heads and smirked, their ponytails scraping their backs.

"Why me?" my uncle said. The power lines moved like arteries over the houses. Like thick roots, they pierced the air.

Because Nykole was always running away from home, her parents took the door to her bedroom off.

"This isn't fair," she said. "When will I get it back?"

"At the end of the school year," said her parents. "If you're good."

"It isn't fair," said Nykole.

At football games the cheerleaders were like grief counselors. In school they moved through the halls in synchronized movements.

My father worked on his glossary.

My Father's Suicide Note

Sisyphus

Chatterton

Plath

Maslow's Pyramid of Needs

Thanatos

Tesla

The high-voltage transmission lines were strung from long ceramic insulators mounted on tall steel towers. My grandmother said, "It's not right." She had run for public office to put regulations on the chemical company. After her third husband asked her to not raise a fuss, she told him to leave, and not come back. "No one talks to me like that," she said. "Raise a fuss? I'll show you what 'raise a fuss' means." Uncle Bob's hunting dog sniffed at the torn screen door. A dead deer stared from the TV—the antlers came out of its brain.

"The single-celled *Paramecia amelia* has eight different sexes," said Mr. Higley with his head lowered. Todd said it must be easy for it to get a date. I never told him about my father. Todd was reading Jack Kerouac. "Perhaps nothing is true but everything is real," he said. "Is that true?" I asked.

"Why am I the one who gets stuck living with a crazy woman?" said Uncle Bob to his hunting dogs. The power lines brought to things an inner light.

Late one night I saw my father's unfinished suicide note sitting on the kitchen table. I couldn't make out the yawning rumpled letters. It was as if a mole had left behind soft indentations and lumps. The *k* was a broken gate. The *j* oozed down the page. His *m* had at least one too many bumps—a humpbacked Bactrian. (Mr. Higley didn't know how they had sex.) The next morning I told my father his handwriting was terrible. After the criticism, he began to take more care with every letter. He was more attentive to the spaces, the line and loop. His *B*'s less plump. His *a* less loopy. Eventually his letters were less smudged—less squished into one another. They squirted out of his pen as his hand floated over the page.

"I stopped taking the pills," said my grandmother. "They were making me a little groggy, but I don't sleep anymore." Uncle Bob watched the hunting channel all day long—men straddling the necks of shot deer, twisting the heads by the antlers until they looked directly into the camera. The commercials sold products that would eliminate the human smell. The antlers were like huge puzzle pieces. "There are mind traps. And body traps. And there are soul traps," said my grandmother. "That's what's your uncle's in."

"What about my father?" I asked.

Nykole said her doorway was like a wound. Like a dowry. At night she dreamt someone was drilling a hole in her skull. In our poetry class, they asked us to write a letter to our favorite poet. Electricity traveled through the power lines as if it were leaving us behind.

The dead deer kept staring from Uncle Bob's TV. My grandmother asked him to change the channel. Uncle Bob reminded her of her campaign lawn signs. "You know the problem with your father, young lady?" Uncle Bob said to me. "He didn't keep busy. You've got to have a hobby."

"Your hobby is killing things," said my grandmother.

"Hey, if you don't direct your attention at something else," said Uncle Bob, "you start looking in the mirror." The dead deer—the antlers like a broken shovel—looked out at him from the TV.

My Father's Suicide Note

For our science project we were supposed to select a source of energy. The cheerleaders selected electricity and they depicted Mixmasters and television sets and electric chairs. Me, Nykole, and Todd did nuclear power. We displayed Little Boy and Fat Man. Our teacher, his tie drizzling down his chest, looked at Todd and said we had made the right decision about who should represent the bomb that fell on Nagasaki.

Todd believed the more syllables a name had, the more feminine that person would be. "John Wayne. Now that was a name. Instead of Marion Morrison." "You mean like Todd Dodd?" asked Nykole. Todd's body looked tender like mud.

The cheerleaders flipped through the air at basketball games as if gravity were useless. Nykole said to her parents, "What are you going to do? Take away my window?"

"I haven't figured it out yet," I heard my father say to my mother.

"What?" she asked.

"What keeps everybody else from killing themselves." In the front yard, snow fell on Elizabeth Hart.

"I understand your father is attempting suicide," said Ms. Abrams, the school counselor.

"Well, I'm not sure I would quite put it that way," I replied.

"Just so you know, Keira," she said. "A higher percentage of girls whose fathers commit suicide have tendencies to be promiscuous."

She must have told my mother, because she started asking me strange questions. "You're not having sex yet, are you? You'll regret it. Once you start in that direction, that's all anyone will want from you."

Uncle Bob said, "Jesus was good at finding the loopholes in this death thing." My grandmother said, "When evil looks like evil, it's bad—but what's worse is evil that doesn't look evil." She had suspected the chemical company had tampered with her election lawn signs. People would ask her, "What does 'Vote for hang' mean? It doesn't sound good."

The cheerleaders climbed each other's bodies. Higher and higher. As if they had this terrible hunger to devour the gymnasium sky. As they rose, they became smaller and more lovely. More lovely and ready to leap out of their bodies.

I bought my father another notebook. "Details," I said. I thought of my English class. "Character development. Motivation."

"What happens," he asked, "when you reach the pinnacle of Maslow's Pyramid of Needs? Self-actualization. Then what? An empty hotel room?"

I left the notebook on the table. My mother was always yelling to keep the house clean. "You can't know when the day will arrive." She called me into her bedroom. "Listen, Kiera," she said. "I think it's my fault. And I can barely live with myself. That's why it's important we do the best we can." I told her I didn't understand. "When you were small, I left him." She said she did come back, of course, but she felt he never did.

"Why did you do that?" asked Nykole as Todd walked out from the middle of the cheerleaders.

I wrote my letter:

Dear Sylvia,

Why did you kill yourself?

My grandmother said, "I blame his father."

"Don't get me wrong," said Uncle Bob. "I don't mind that he's writing it. I just think he's pretty selfish if he thinks we are supposed to read it."

My Father's Suicide Note

The power lines leaked into our houses. My grandmother's dining room table was piled with the unopened merchandise from the time when she used to shoplift. Cans of vegetables from the grocery store. Containers of condoms, like packets of tea, from the drugstore. Tubes of breath mints from the gas station.

"Males are like vacuum cleaners," Nykole said to Todd. "They come with attachments." Todd, his flesh like porridge, looked like a missionary. Fat and kind. And afraid that what he had been seeking was a lie. Nykole said she felt as if she were living in a dollhouse with one wall entirely missing. She felt there were parts of her life completely exposed. Todd announced that he was going to run away from home. "Don't be silly," I said. "I don't think any of us really has a home."

Our English teacher asked us to pull out our thesauruses. I shared Nykole's, and Todd asked, "What's another word for 'thesaurus'?" For a week, we studied the conditional clause. The cheerleaders chanted:

> If Todd Dodd
> thinks he's God,
> all he is
> is really odd.

Uncle Bob talked about "those people" and said that he wasn't going to waste his time planting corn.

My grandmother saw the dead deer on the hunting channel get up on rickety card-table legs and hobble right out of the TV. It had a careful bullet hole in its chest. The deer tilted forward under the weight of its antlers. The chandelier of bone. As if the deer were balancing a transmission tower on its head. It stepped over the hassock and tip-hoofed around some dining room chairs, which were gathered around the table piled with a small hill of formerly shoplifted merchandise, and walked through the door, clattering over the porch. My grandmother took this as a sign.

The cheerleaders bled into each other. Prim and polished. Their mild contained enthusiasm stretched over events like skin. When Todd looked at them, he imagined a pyramid of *W*'s shattering into broken *M*'s. When he explained this to Ms. Abrams, she had him expelled from school.

Mr. Actaeon, our history teacher, said it was getting more and more difficult for him to separate history from myth. Todd's seat was empty.

The day arrived when I had to ask my father, "So, how do you intend to do it?" He looked concerned, as if he'd never thought of it before.

Nykole was right about the breast thing. And Todd said, "Ah, com'on." Nykole said she dug a cave in back of her bedroom and practiced dancing. As we brushed the weather out of our hair, Nykole said she didn't think she would ever have sex—at least not that way. She said she would probably live in another country when she grew up and that she would invite me and we would step out onto a veranda and dance. Todd told us he would be moving away, and he said, "Ah, com'on."

VOTE FOR TRANSFORMATION, the revised lawn sign read.

My father attended the Health and Human Sexuality end-of-the-year display. Nykole's parents were there—her mother smelling like hair spray and menthol cigarettes, and her father with gray accountant's hair. They were carrying her bedroom door. The cheerleaders spun like pinwheels above the displays, which stretched all the way around the gym. Bonobo chimps and insects and dolphins stared ecstatically from poster boards as students did elaborate demonstrations. Some of the inhabitants of Warners were openly offended. Everything was connected through the bracelet of sex.

My father stood in front of my display. I had prepared a series of pictures. Dragonflies emitted a secretion bonding the pair together. They flew off, mating in midair. "It must be beautiful," my father said. And he started to cry. "I had no idea."

My grandmother stood in the middle of the chemical waste site under the terrible hum of the power lines. Uncle Bob, with the ointment on his body that didn't allow him to smell like a human being, was out target shooting when he saw her scattering the corn. "What are you doing here? People know you're crazy. You are a crazy old woman," he said as his hunting dogs growled and he waved his rifle like a conductor's baton. But my grandmother ignored him, kernels showering from her fingers. And then it happened. The corn broke through the earth and instantaneously grew. Stalks gripped the husks like candles, and husks cupped their gold insides. Alleys of corn surrounded my grandmother. Canals of corn. And when Uncle Bob, standing under the power lines and staring at the field of new corn, described it to Sheriff Wilby, Uncle Bob said he had never seen anything like it.

Because it was the last day of school, I was excited and couldn't sleep. When I came downstairs, I saw my father. He sat alone and luminous at the kitchen table. I looked through the layers of him. It was as if he had once been my father—and now was someone else. "What's another word for 'home'?" he asked. I wasn't even sure he knew me. "How's it going?" I said. He answered, "Now I get to the hard part."

Patrick Lawler

SCUBA DIVER FOUND IN MIDDLE
OF FOREST FIRE

1.

After the "incident," Mr. Hyde hasn't been quite right. No one can determine what it is exactly. It appears something has bitten him—but no one knows what. They only know he isn't the same—though no one remembers what "the same" really is. He loses things. Speech. Feelings in his limbs. The ability to do whatever he has done. It is like he gets tired of looking. In the faded squashed couch, he tilts into the TV. When I talk to Matt, the father fearfully examines his son's mouth.

2.

First, I want to say I don't think it is fair that I haven't gotten better grades in this course. I mean, it's Introductory Journalism. I want to say that I don't intend to make a career out of newspaper writing. But I do need a C if I am going to get through this semester. I don't think I suck with details and description. I know how to tell a story.

3.

Mr. Hyde looks at everything as if it were about to hurt him. The TV light bathes his eyeball. See.

4.

Mr. Hyde's son works as an orderly in a hospital—and now has his own apartment. His name is Matt. Before the mysterious bite incident, the father used to say, "That's no job for a man. Hauling shit in a bedpan. You'd never find me doing that. Working in a loony bin." Things are different now.

My father must feel the saliva of a strange beast bathe his brain. He must drink in the mind of the forest.

5.

Matt wants to take his father back to the lake at the center of the woods. "There's something mystical going on, in a creepy way," he says. "I think he needs to get in touch with what is killing him." Mrs. Hyde says, "I wish he had never come out of the woods. The way he is, and all."

6.

It is easy to become the thing you are afraid of. At least that's what Cayla says. The TV light brands Mr. Hyde's face while the news reports announce torture and chemical spills and burning and bad weather. I feel a little uncomfortable being here.

7.

Mrs. Hyde has the presence of a Styrofoam cup. I'm not saying that in an entirely negative way.

He pulls the whole night sky up close to his face.

8.

My father, who is a volunteer fireman, was called to the scene. We are neighbors of the Hydes. When they found Mr. Hyde, no one recognized the teeth marks on his arm, so later they asked the veterinarian. He held the punctured arm under the lamp and shook his head. "It doesn't look good," he said to Mrs. Hyde. My father stood, with his psoriasis pink skin, which in an odd way makes him look youthful.

9.

Cayla (do I need to mention she's the girl I'm seeing?) says her mother once took her to a healer. Cayla remembers the terribleness of healing. She remembers one person crying her new eyes out. She remembers almost feeling like she could fly.

10.

On the TV, the televangelist kindles—sputters. Mr. Hyde jerks back.

11.

When they discovered him beside the woods under the barbed wire, no one wanted to touch him. There was that kind of strangeness in his eyes. They were afraid that whatever he had seen was contagious. Then they found the bite marks.

He looks like he is in pain—as if he feels the back of his eyes crack.

12.

I ask Mrs. Hyde why Mr. Hyde had gone into the woods.

"He'd been behaving strangely."

"But what was he doing there?" I ask.

"He was always looking for something—something that wasn't his life."

Her eyes freeze around the nothing she is looking at. "Something that wasn't me."

13.

For months no one in the area goes into the woods, just in case something bad might happen.

14.

I know some people say we have to get close to nature—but my father tells me this story. Once a scuba diver's body was found in the middle of a California forest fire. What was he doing there? Supposedly, when the helicopter scooped up a bucket of water from the ocean to dump on the fire, it inadvertently took up the scuba diver.

That's what happens when we find ourselves in places we shouldn't be.

15.

I think I wouldn't mind being a wild life biologist.

My father's central nervous system must be attached to the ancient stars as his mind digs through an old order to an even older darkness.

16.

If it weren't for this assignment—Profile a Person—I wouldn't talk to Matt. He is just too weird. He wears a black T-shirt that says THINK—IT'S NOT ILLEGAL YET. I turn on the tape recorder, and he starts talking about making a bed without disturbing the patient. "Folding and unfolding. The body, rolled like a log, disappears inside the white cocoon of sheets, and then reappears out of the whiteness—as if it had come out the other side of something." It is like he is trying to make a point about something that doesn't have a point. That's when I want to direct him to his T-shirt, but I think better of it. That's when I say, "I'm here to write about your father."

17.

I can't imagine interviewing people for a living. Why would I want the opinion of someone who knows less than I do?

18.

Cayla says the bed thing sounds important. Like a metaphor. When she was young, her legs were crooked. Now she is an English major. She's always seeing significance where there isn't any. That's the great thing about journalism. You're trained not to see significance anywhere. Just information.

A forgotten gland vibrates between being mind and being body.

19.

Cayla asks me what animal I would be, and she says she would be a bird. And I say I wouldn't mind flying, but I have somewhat lower aspirations.

"Maybe I'd be a fly."

"Com'on," she says. And I say a horse.

And she says, "Why not combine them and be a horsefly?" I laugh.

20.

Mrs. Hyde walks around with a sponge. She has an odd-shaped head. I've seen pictures of heads in my psychology textbook. Head maps that locate where the brain thinks and feels.

21.

I think I wouldn't mind being a forensic psychologist. I mean, if the horsefly thing doesn't work out.

22.

"Hydrophobia," the veterinarian says. "That's what they used to call it. Don't let Mr. Hyde go near water."

23.

"In a very real sense the animal is still getting to know my father."

Mr. Hyde's son has some very strange ideas. He dropped out of college about a year ago. I think it was drugs. And he says he writes poetry, and I tell him I'm just taking notes for an assignment about his father.

The mysterious animal is still in the woods.

24.

Here's a joke from class that not many people seem to get. What do you call a reporter's notes? Evidence.

25.

Cayla talks to me about my own father. She says, "I'll bet every time your father enters a burning house, it must be like he is entering his own death."

And I say, "He doesn't do it that often."

I tell my father this, and he looks strange and says, "Every time I enter any house I imagine what it would look like in flames."

25.

After I'm done interviewing him, Matt sends me an e-mail.

He works on a psychiatric floor in the local hospital. When we were growing up, I frankly didn't have much to do with him.

26.

Cayla says the scuba diver must have been totally shocked. My father, who looks a lot younger than he is, says he's not going to pay for any course I don't pass.

27.

Why is Matt e-mailing Cayla? If you ask me, they should compare the bite mark on the father's arm with the teeth in the son's mouth. Matt tells me I can't use his words in my article. I tell him not to worry, but I'll find a way.

Nothing stands between its brain and his. Nothing stands between its mouth and my father's blood.

Patrick Lawler

28.

I suppose the animal still moves somewhere inside the forest. Pictures would be helpful here, but of course I won't have any. I imagine the middle of the woods is a dark, churning place. Cayla says what Matt writes is like poetry, and I say, "Right." And I say if it is that good, I'll use it in my assignment. "But he doesn't want you to" is all Cayla says.

29.

Maybe Mr. Hyde just needs to look out a window. Maybe his son needs to get a life.

30.

I suppose good things happen—like the forest fire eventually gets put out. But then when you look really close, you see there's a scuba diver who, with all the amount of swimming in the world, can't possibly save himself.

31.

I feel sorry for Mr. Hyde with a son like Matt. The father topples into the jerking TV light. It almost bruises him. His head seems to be swimming inside it. I think I wouldn't mind being a phrenologist.

I'm sure there's something out there trying to explain us. The one who is inside my father now. The one who my father is becoming. The mysterious animal is still in the words.

Patrick Lawler

THE DOOR-TO-DOOR DOOR SALESMAN

"When the door of opportunity knocks . . ." said my boss and his voice trailed off. I was just glad to have a job. I'd walk up to a house and knock at a door or ring a doorbell and the resident would come and answer it and say, "Can I help you?" And I'd go, "I couldn't help but notice that you could use a new door."

Of course, all of this happened before the water came in such large amounts that it altered our lives, and everything we thought we understood became submerged beneath everything we feared.

My sister was afraid that something bad would happen to her fetus. Bobby, the guy who lived with her, worked in the Life Science Lab. He'd put his hand on my sister's belly and go, "Everything's fine as far as I can tell."

"You're so stupid," said Amy. "I can't believe you don't know what is happening."

As Bobby walked across the parking lot, he could see a primitive light from deep within the lab.

———————

"We must prepare ourselves for something good to happen," said my mother as she arranged the self-help books in the display shelves at the entrance of the library.

———————

My father, rumpled and distant, was a science teacher in the middle school. When my sister told him she was pregnant, he was preparing his class. He stood with one hand attached to a generator and the other to a fluorescent lightbulb. My sister was afraid of my father when he prepared his class on lightning.

"Maybe I can bring you to school," he said to Amy. "To illustrate a point."

The fluorescent light burned bright in his hand. When I was young, I believed he was holding his brain. As if the light were something his body were thinking. As if the light were what his body shed.

"Listen, Amy, I'm going to prepare the biggest experiment my students have ever seen."

———————

Once Bobby said to my sister, while grabbing clumps of clothes from the hamper, "I know it sounds strange, but there's something I really like about a Laundromat. The hum and gush. Really. The shimmering insides of the driers. The clean smell of everything. It's the waiting that I love. If you want to know the truth."

———————————————

"At least he helps you," said my mother.

"I feel useless." My sister sat with my mother in the living room. "I feel like I'm inside the fetus," said my sister.

———————————————

"It's not like I want to. I mean, who would want to? All the noise. It's like working in an insane asylum. You wouldn't believe the screeching. You can't even hear yourself not think," said Bobby. His laminated eyes stared from the ID clipped to the pocket of his uniform.

"You got to understand," he said as he folded a pile of laundry while Amy bulged on the bed. "It's not like they're real monkeys. They're lab monkeys. They were bred for experimentation. They wouldn't have even been alive, for godssake, if it weren't for what we need to do to them. And really we don't even have a choice, if you think about it. Either we try to cure things and do this—or we just die from things we don't have to die from—just so something else lives. What kind of thing is that?"

"All's I know," said my sister, "is that I think I'm feeling this thing run under my skin."

"What thing?"

"The monkeys. I don't know. What they are feeling."

"That's crazy."

"Maybe. But it's affecting me—and your baby. You've got to stop, is all I'm saying."

Most people were polite. I'd usually touch the door and say, "You know what would look good here?" I'm tempted to say they slammed the door in my face—but it was usually closed with a more muffled, almost apologetic sound. "Sorry," they'd say as the final crack between the door and the frame quietly vanished.

My father called himself a psychopractor. "A manipulator of the brain," he'd explain. "A chiropractor of the mind."

"You're an eighth-grade science teacher," said my mother. Her years as the town librarian affected the volume of her voice. She always spoke in a muffled whisper, so when she said something, everything appeared to tilt toward her.

There was never any indication that the weather was about to change. Or even that it wasn't. My father studied the weather woman on Channel 7 as she leaned into a front. It was as if the weather came out of her hands.

My mother sat at the kitchen table, arranging all the names of people who had overdue books. "I just don't understand how people can be so irresponsible." She held Bobby's card in her hand. It said *How to Respond to Your Wife's Pregnancy,* with an almost illegible blue date beside it.

"What point?" my sister asked our father.

"Consequences," our father replied. His hand touched my sister's belly, and the fluorescent lightbulb jerked and flickered in his hand.

Bobby saved change in a pickle jar. He said to Amy, "You know if we keep saving quarters, when the baby's our age, can you imagine how much we'll have to give him?"

"Her," said Amy.

"No, that's not what I wanted," said my father to his class as the children dragged garbage bags behind them. "I wanted to know how much human waste we produce—how much bodily waste. Sleep in the eyes in the morning. Ear wax. Eyelashes left on your pillow."

The Door-to-Door Salesman

My father became obsessed with bodily litter. Urine and feces, of course, but he was concerned with everything from menstrual blood to saliva.

"It's just that I need to know," he said to my mother while he measured out his fingernails on a scale.

He kept his hair when it was cut.

Tears and skin.

Amy said to Bobby, "Don't listen to my brother. He's always making things up."

Bobby announced that at the diner they had wings for sale.

"What do they do at Life Science?" I asked Bobby.

"I'm not sure. But as for me, security. Basically, check doors."

"It's not your baby," my sister said to Bobby. She turned to me, "I sometimes feel the electrodes attached to their brains."

Bobby looked at me as if he wanted me to say something.

"Wings sound good to me," I said.

I walked up the porch steps, carrying my door, and I heard music coming from inside. A woman was behind the front door when it opened. I didn't know what to say. From that point on she became the woman with the singing door.

Bobby said, "One day when we cure cancer, then you'll thank me."

"Bobby, you're a security guard," said Amy.

My father said, "I give them wonder."

"Who?" asked my sister.

"The students."

Amy said she could feel the monkeys' pain right down inside the fetus.

If they let me in, I had a pamphlet with all these shiny doors, aching to be opened. I spread them out on the coffee tables until they looked like tiny trap doors into the customers' basements.

Frequently, when I was in the midst of all these "splendidly depicted portals," with their brass handles and eager knockers, they showed me a more real door.

"They've got to get used to losing their bodies," said my father.

"Hey, it's Life Science, not Death Science," said Bobby.

"That's eagle knocker, not eager knocker," said my boss.

The Door-to-Door Salesman

"Come on," said Bobby. "I'm not responsible. You can't blame me. Someone's got to put food on our table. I wasn't the one who went and got pregnant. What do you want me to do—sell doors with your brother?"

Sometimes he hated to hear the animals. Once when he got drunk, he told me he was going to get a book to help him get through this.

"See my mother," I said.

My boss said, "You've got to ask yourself what makes this door better than any other door. It's got to be more than functionality. More than even aesthetics. More than the golden flying knockers. You got to make them see that this door—and only this door—opens up into their new life. It is possibility. It is hope. On one side of this door is your customer's new self. On this side is you. This is your door of opportunity. Knock on it, and it will open." He held up the sample door. "I'm serious," he said. "Knock on it."

I formed a reluctant fist and the middle knuckle lightly tapped on the wood.

"Keep knocking and one day—who knows—you'll be like me. The Huxley door," he said. "There's nothing like it."

Whenever my father placed the scales on the dining room table, we winced—uncertain about what he was preparing to weigh.

———————————

"You're not framing the product correctly," said my boss. "I mean. You've got to make them want it. Pamphlets only present an entrance into their hungers. They need the real thing. The entrée."

Following his advice, I started carrying the door down the street.

———————————

From porch to porch I trod, the door precariously balanced on my back, shielding me from the sun but also creating beneath it a dark crypt—a portable room I carried through the town.

I moved inside this shadow pocket and thought about the woman with the singing door.

———————————

Bobby once said, "I know what it is. It is exactly the same kind of light that comes from the Laundromat as comes from the Life Science Lab. A clean light."

———————————

The Door-to-Door Salesman

I got my hopefulness from my mother. I could barely hear her when she spoke, so I leaned in close to her desk. "With all of the despair in the world and the pain and the suffering, it is absolutely amazing it could all be turned into this." Her hand swept from the stacks of fiction to the intimidating reference books and landed on her display of self-help paperbacks. Her voice lowered and though I could barely hear her, I knew she intended what she said to be of critical importance. I leaned in close and heard her say, "This is the essayists of the human spearfish." I could have asked her to repeat it, but she announced it with such conviction that I knew my inability to have grasped it in its entirety would have disappointed her.

———————

At first we didn't know how much it rained, and then we could not imagine our world without water. When we went to bed, we were puddles; when we woke up, we were a lake. The power lines dragged. The cars were sunk in water up to the wipers. The mailman almost drowned with his waterlogged sack. "Where did all the water come from?" asked Bobby.

My father watched the weather woman on Channel 7, as real water engulfed the lower half of her map.

———————

"What am I supposed to do?" I asked, looking at the Huxley leaning against my chair. "Who's going to want a door now?"

"People more than ever are going to want to keep things out. Wherever they have one door, now they'll want two." He spoke into a small stack of wet contracts. "Everything is an opportunity to sell something. Boy, if you are going to make it in this world, you've got to remember that."

There was no acceptable explanation for the flood. "Invisible rain," said the mayor.

"Residual biblical activity," explained the minister.

"Reverse virga," said the weather woman on Channel 7, and my father looked confused.

"Subterranean leakage," said Bobby's father, who was a plumber. "It was bound to happen," he said to Bobby. "All the pipes and tunnels and estuaries and storm drains. All the liquid striations. The drunken subductions. What did anyone expect?"

As Bobby slogged through the street with his basket of clothes, a fertile light came from deep within the Laundromat.

They asked my father to take water samples. He confirmed that what was around us was indeed water—only at catastrophic levels.

The barber's pole stuck out of the water like one of our father's fluorescent bulbs gone crazy. The town's one traffic light bobbed like a buoy—the red half-dunked.

"We couldn't have gone on that way forever," said Bobby's father, his plunger over his shoulder.

My sister fell into a grave depression. Her hair started falling out. And Bobby's father was always in their apartment, unclogging sinks.

The skin of water grew over everything.

My sister said, "What is going to happen to the animals locked in their cages?"

My father said, "It is getting hard to tell where the body ends and the water begins." His scale floated away.

My mother stared at Bobby's library card. She looked at Bobby's name tag. His eyes stared fearfully from above his name, Bobby Tibbles. My mother's eyes went from the library card to the name tag to Bobby's face.

"I thought the book would have helped," said Bobby, tapping the purple book jacket with the picture of somebody else. "It didn't. It's probably me. I'm not a fast reader." The water in front of the desk was up to Bobby's ankles.

"If the water gets any higher, I'm afraid the books will float away," said my mother to one of Bobby's faces.

"Do you want me to call my father?" asked Bobby.

Eventually my sister told me she was afraid of what was growing inside her. "I look in the mirror and all I see are monkeys with their prune-colored hair. Their baby faces."

"I'm going to save them," she told my mother.

If there had been sad rainy weather, it would have been understandable.

The Laundromat opened all its silvery underfed mouths. The water opened its dark belly. My father stood with a gleaming baton in his hand. It was as if the electricity were coming from his pulse. His harvest of light. "You'll get electrocuted," said my mother.

The minister talked about a "terrible cleansing." The mayor spoke about "developmental opportunities." The weather woman on Channel 7 said there was a "topical depression," as she gleamed in front of my father.

The Door-to-Door Salesman

Early in the morning at the obliterated corners of the town, lines of schoolchildren with their backpacks strapped to them like life jackets filled with bricks swam conscientiously to school. My father often wondered what kept the children afloat during his experiments and lectures. He told them there had occurred an alteration of physics or gravity, he wasn't sure. "Whatever it is, it makes all my knowledge obsolete. I have nothing left to teach you. Now you must listen to your own bodies."

My father felt there had been something missing. "Eventually the placenta," said my father. "It will have to be weighed."

"We are all trapped behind something beautiful," said my mother when Amy said she was asking Bobby to leave. Before he left, Amy took his keys. "I can't take it any longer. The defilement of their sweet brains."

With a pickle jar in his lap and a fistful of change, Bobby sat in the Laundromat, every washer and dryer spinning and humming numbly with a silvery nothingness inside them.

He hovered between the driers on one side and the washers on the other. Between the piles of dark and the bump of blank whites. As if he were somehow in the belly of a purring creature.

Patrick Lawler

Amy started dragging my doors out of the basement and into the water. "What do you think you are doing?" I asked. "You'll hurt yourself."

I wanted to see the woman with the singing door—but now I had no excuse.

My father's students were afraid to weep because then they would have to weigh the tears.

My mother was trying desperately to keep the books from floating away, though one book by Melville escaped. I wanted to ask my mother what she meant by the essayists of the human spearfish but the timing wasn't right.

My father and mother sat on the front porch as a book floated by. "It got away," my mother said.

"Don't worry," said my father. It was nearly dark and we could hardly see, but it appeared as if a fleet of Huxley doors drifted past our house. And if you had a really good imagination, you might have thought you saw scared chimps, with electric yarmulkes and dangling wires, huddled around the golden knockers and clinging to each other.

The Door-to-Door Salesman

"I really did think that something good would happen—but now that it hasn't, we must prepare ourselves for something else," said my mother in a low, determined whisper. My father touched my mother's hand and rubbed it lovingly and curiously, looking intently at whether any of my mother's skin came off on his hands.

Patrick Lawler

AT ONE OF MY FATHER'S FUNERALS, I WAS HUMPHREY BOGART

At one of my father's funerals, I was Humphrey Bogart. I stood in a trench coat, pulling the smoke out of a cigarette. At one of my father's funerals, he was very talkative—almost inappropriately so. "It is amazing," he said. "You just wouldn't believe it."

At one of my father's funerals, my mother danced. Awkwardly at first, nearly toppling, then eventually she moved, as graceful as fog. At first her foot seemed to test the solidness of the floor, and then came the tentative attempts. Finally, to the dismay of my aunts, she twirled dreamily, like an Arthur Murray dance instructor in a trance.

At one of my father's funerals, we all fell asleep. An elderly lady gently snored to the rhythm of barely audible church hymns.

At one of my father's funerals, the servants brought in delicious bowls of fruit, and we wept like gods.

At one of my father's funerals, all we could do was talk about Shelley's heart.

At One of my Father's Funerals, I was Humphrey Bogart

At one of my father's funerals, a woman appeared with scratches on her hands from having tried to catch too many birds. At one of my father's funerals, a child bored breathing holes into the casket. At one of my father's funerals, the river cracked through the walls—fish leapt into the coffin.

At one of my father's funerals, he poked his head through a portal. "Now anything is possible," he said.

At one of my father's funerals, Jesus showed up—tortured and celestial. The synchronized weepers' choreographed tears fell like musical notes.

At one of my father's funerals, he said, "What do I hear for this lovely casket? Barely used."

A man in a grayish robe raised his hand. "Jesus," I said.

At one of my father's funerals, I was older than my father. "You look like hell," he said.

At one of my father's funerals, we thought my uncle brought flowers, but it was really a rash. One of my aunts came with an alibi.

My father said, "If I am not conscious of my death, then how can I be dead?"

The doctor listed the symptoms and pushed his finger into my father's chest in order to find the heart.

At one of my father's funerals, the bounty hunter wept into his warrant. A fisherman laid a whimsical fish on the coffin. At one of my father's funerals, a fire started. The tow truck driver arrived with the flowers. At one of my father's funerals, the funeral director dipped a cigarette into embalming fluid. The driver of the hearse was picked up for DWI. The bootlegger comforted me. "They'll never be anyone like your father," he said.

At one of my father's funerals, the tour bus came in with the Alzheimer's patients, who were trying to say the right words to the family. The stroke patients tilted beautifully in their card table chairs.

At one of my father's funerals, I developed the power to exchange organs with my dying relatives. When I left the room, I had the liver of a drunken uncle. At one of my father's funerals, we read the Romantics, and Keats showed up. At one of my father's funerals, I cried, and no one asked me why.

At one of my father's funerals, a man carried an umbrella. A woman carried a packed suitcase. My father announced that he was afraid of falling.

I watched a tear roll down the umbrella.

At one of my father's funerals, we played cards while my father sat in his mahogany drawer. While he was trying to untie the knot in his head, my mother deposited her voice in the cochlea of his ear. The priest said, "Now what are we going to do?"

A girl announced she had had a dream about a traveling funeral.

I pondered a handful of birds.

At one of my father's funerals, Katharine Hepburn showed up. Her beauty seared our brains. A big bold hat tipped over her eye. She had orchid shimmer on her lips.

At one of my father's funerals, a woman showed me her hands and said, "This is what happens when you try to catch birds." I was an adolescent. I announced to the girl, "I keep a book called *Magic* under my bed."

At one of my father's funerals, someone mentioned the frozen dream where all the dream characters are trapped behind a thin layer of ice. Eventually we rowed the coffin across the lake. At one of my father's funerals, my mother inconsolably danced.

Patrick Lawler

MY SISTER'S FAKE WEDDING GOWN

I.

summer

My sister's fake wedding dress hung like lichen in the front closet, next to my fake graduation gown.

As the town sheriff, my father kept meticulous records, intricate charts showing all the interconnections—how people's lives intertwined—sheets of paper with dates and names and locations filling tiny circles and connected with short curving lines. Like weather maps. Delicate pencil-drawn webs eventually to be used as evidence.

People stopped by our home with bags full of information, and my mother would take them to her part of the house.

When my grandfather died, my mother had an addition built, so our grandmother could move in. Artemis Hitch owned his own carpenter's business, and my mother worked out an agreement by which she did his bookkeeping and his taxes in exchange for his labor. My grandmother said to my sister, "Amy, I can't get his death out of me."

My father said, "Do not play in the backyard while they're building. There are nails in those boards. Rusty. Sharp. And if you step on one, you'll get lockjaw."

Amy was going to college in the fall. "We'll see what happens," said my father. She was going to live at home for the first year. At least, that's what my father said.

"You just have to admire all the possibilities," he said as he looked at his charts. "All the opportunities. All the motives. All the lovely deceptions."

My father was known for his interrogating abilities. My sister and I—and to some extent even our mother—feared it when he would ask us questions. And after we'd answer, he'd take out his charts, unroll them in front of us, and we knew we were dead. We knew we couldn't be at a friend's house if our friend was visiting a sick aunt.

We would get confused about the times when things happened. We'd stumble when asked about what somebody said or where somebody was. While we'd get tangled in the vines of each other, he always knew how to unknot us. The whole town rolled out before us, and we knew we were dead.

"Knowledge is key," he said. "Knowing the details. Getting at the bottom of things. It's what will eventually ensnare you." He looked at each of us across the dining room table.

"Watch how you answer his questions" was what my sister used to say to me.

It was always best to have an alibi.

I felt the nail penetrate the rubber sole of the sneaker like a spike going through a slab of liver, and, at that moment, I knew my life would be altered.

I kept opening my jaw, making certain it didn't get stuck. I didn't know what lockjaw was, but I was certain I had it. Whatever had been waiting in the nail was waiting in my blood.

My father's charts grew into tangled globes. My sister was going to start taking an ecology class at the local college and was letting her boyfriend touch her breasts.

After the addition went up, my grandmother brought fat potted flowers. I knew it was fall when their jaws fell off.

II.

fall

The wound at the bottom of my foot grew red.

"Ecology," Amy repeated to our grandmother when she again asked what Amy was studying.

My grandmother would say to my sister, "I'll never live long enough to see you get married." Or she'd say to me, "I'll never live long enough to see you graduate." Or she'd say to my mother, "I'll never live long enough to see you happy."

My father questioned my sister about her relationship with her boyfriend.

Eventually the wound at the bottom of my foot closed up—but the fear only increased. The poison that had been deposited in the hole had no way to get out. It would travel up my bloodstream until it would reach my mouth.

My Sister's Fake Wedding Gown

One night I came down from my bedroom, and I saw my sister quickly pull down her sweater over her boyfriend's hand.

My father always asked, "What are you doing?" and we'd always answer, "Nothing."

My mother decided that to reduce our grandmother's concern about not being present at future family experiences, we as a family would create what she announced would be preemptive events. "If she can't be in the future, then we'll simply bring the future to her."

"Kind of like a rehearsal," said Amy.

"Kind of like a run-through before the commission of a crime," said my father.

"It's really a lie," I said.

"Let's think of them as prematurely real events," said my mother. "And Gramma won't ever have to know."

"It means 'the study of home,'" my sister said to my grandmother, who was pouring some tea in a cup.

"Well, since you went off to college, I don't see you much around your *own* home anymore." Our grandmother placed a rose-decorated cup in the rose-decorated saucer. "It can't be much of a course."

With a combination of relief and anxiety, Artemis Hitch, moisture glistening his eyes, placed his ledgers in front of my mother. Her clients came to her with tremendous remorse. Either they felt regret for making too little money or felt guilt for making too much. Their arms full of facts, they carried their dependents, their contributions, their dividends like boulders. The stacks of bills, the bank statements and check stubs, the tattered receipts—these were portions of a secret code clients entrusted to my mother. "Accountability," said my father when he'd see the clients exit my mother's office. Their worries set adrift on my mother's desk, they refused to let my father interfere with their sense of relief.

All that fall I sat opening my jaw in math class. Cloudy messages from all the previous classes poked through the smudged blackboard. A palimpsest. I looked at the world through exhaust.

"So what's his name?" said my father. "Brian," said my sister.

"Amy, what would a person do who studies ecology? I don't believe I ever knew anybody who did that." Our grandmother's fingers drummed the table. "But I can never figure out what your mother does either."

During the tax season, my mother prepared the forms of the entire town, and for the rest of the year she kept the books of the shopkeepers and the business owners. She did the payrolls and the quarterly reports.

"I'll never live long enough to see you get married," said my grandmother to Amy.

My grandmother's things began to occupy more and more space in our house. She talked to Amy the night before her fake wedding. "You didn't really know your grandfather and me. I mean we were married, but we were so different. We barely talked. But you get used to it. Marriage is like two different species living together."

"Like lichen," said Amy. My grandmother looked puzzled. "It's fungus and algae growing together. Symbiotically."

"Symbolically, all I know, Amy, is I wasn't the fungus."

"Do you take this woman to be your fake bride?" said the forlorn man on the altar.

Standing in my rented tux, I asked my sister if she knew anything about lockjaw.

"You're just like a fake son to me," said my father to his fake son-in-law. And then he turned to me and asked, "Why are you doing that with your mouth?"

III.

winter

My sister's false pregnancy was going along nicely. My mother was ecstatic, my grandmother was blissful, my father was preoccupied. "The fake father," he claimed, "has to take some responsibility."

We could hear my mother's adding machine as it gulped down numbers.

From January until April 15, my mother, monk-like, prepared taxes late at night, pounding her typewriter keys until she would finally bang the stapler shut over the W-2s, and she would emerge as if from a spiritual ordeal. During those months, the family had to make an appointment to see her.

While my mother conducted her interviews and prepared the income taxes of the town, my father sat in an adjacent room. That's how he constructed his charts. He would emerge with detailed information. "Don't tell your mother," he'd tell us. "This is the way it has to be. And it is better if she doesn't know."

Because the light was heavier in my mother's office, I always felt it was a separate part of the house. The fluorescent lamp on her desk first came on as if the light were being choked.

"Maybe it's me," my sister said, "but the fake events always seem more cathartic."

I moved my mouth in order to know. I hid my wound in my shoe because I couldn't bear my father's questioning.

The townspeople brought their bags of numbers. Like secrets. Like regrets. They felt an incredible relief when they would give them to my mother.

As she presented her renderings of their financial lives, my father charted their baser instincts and fixations. He understood the deeper meaning behind the receipt for the motel room. He knew the guilt gifts. The complexities of motive were hidden behind numerical fictions. The town shrunk to fit inside his diagrams. His charts were ethical allegories, abstract clouds of connection and moral paradox. The intimations. The scandals. The false alibis. The tangled webs of deception.

The town visited my mother the way some societies go to a shaman. They approached with gratitude and even reverence. My mother in her room of tax codes and adding machines and typewriters was a healer, while my father in his efforts to gather evidence was an opener of wounds. He stood on the periphery, a decipherer of the deepest riddles, capturing the darker nuances of the town until they were transfigured in his webs.

In the winter the roads of the town flowed white like my mother's adding machine tape.

The problem with inviting the people of the town to our fake events was that they got confused.

My math teacher was not pleased to be invited to my graduation party. "He's in seventh grade. Aren't they jumping the gun?" he reportedly asked. "And to be honest, all the boy does is sit in class with his mouth wide open. I expect him to have a question—hopefully an answer—but nothing ever comes out."

I drifted through the room like a shadow in my graduation gown. My math teacher handed me his gift. Remembering the nail, I instinctively pulled back. A sharpened end poked through the wrapping paper as he handed the gift to me.

My sister asked my mother if she should return the wedding gifts. "Well, don't be too hasty," said my mother. "Certainly return the ones you'll never use."

My sister named her fake child Brian. And my father suddenly understood.

IV.

spring

Eventually all the air in the house belonged to my grandmother.

In the closet, my fake graduation gown hung like the shadow of my sister's fake wedding dress.

My mother complained, "We always approach the fake events more seriously than the real ones." Her file cabinets bulged with the town's hopes and debts.

My sister said, "Maybe it's because once you've gone through it, the fake event becomes more real than the real one. And it's the real event that seems fake."

My father thought that made sense.

My grandmother, lifting a cup of tea to her lips, said she would never live long enough for my father to receive the kind of accolades he deserved. That's when we decided to have his fake funeral.

The irony is that the town, which so implicitly trusted my mother to accurately calculate what they owed, feared my father's skill at twisting out the deeper truths in order to determine what more needed to be given.

"Sometimes when you search through the rubble, you can't locate all the evidence. That's what I'm doing now," my father said. "Examining clues before they are relevant. It's not easy connecting the dots before there are dots to connect."

The town slept in the webs my father assembled.

When income tax season was over, I asked my mother if she knew anything about lockjaw. She said it sounded terrible and she wouldn't ever want to have it.

My sister was concerned that the fake events had become substitutes for reality. Because they occurred, was her theory, there was no longer any need for the real event to follow. Then my sister explained the concept of community succession.

The funeral director and the florist were two of my mother's clients.

We placed my father's charts above the coffin. We suspended them from string and they dizzily twisted. They had grown into complicated dance steps that no one could follow. They had evolved into the migration patterns of birds, into immense global conspiratorial theories that no one could ever decipher. The hopelessly complicated became the seamlessly integrated. They revealed the space just beneath reality, where everything is intimately connected.

Some of the people of the town were upset with what they said were the implied accusations of my father—but, considering the situation, how could they not forgive him?

My father's charts, which had always seemed terribly dark and accusatory, now, because they were so elaborately complex, seemed to lose all connection to the real. They were delicate, diaphanous assemblings. Ethereal floating islands, they presented a secret life, one that existed independent of the actual world. Out of my father's ponderous activity, there emerged something like hopefulness. Out of his dark delvings beneath the skin of numbers, a lightness emerged that spoke about our longings and belongings, about our loves and acquaintances, and how we are all tenuously and tenderly shackled together.

When my math teacher saw my father's diagrams, he complimented me for sharing the gift he had given me for graduation. "You know, the compass . . . for drawing arcs. Circles. I can see your father must have used it."

Artemis Hitch said my father actually looked better now that he wasn't so intent on catching someone doing something wrong. Artemis looked up at the charts. "It must have been a relief for him to finally share these terrible things."

Brian, who didn't come around the house anymore, foraged among the funeral home's remembrance cards. "Look," he said to Amy. "They're all different. Different names. Like they're leftovers." Amy quieted him down. "I don't believe it," he said. "This is just unbelievable." We knew the town would have to prepare itself for an immense disappointment.

It had been nearly a year after the nail had entered my foot, and I was relieved. Either the opening and closing of my mouth had prevented lockjaw—or I never had it to begin with, which I seriously doubted. Either way, I felt compelled to continue my activity, at least a little while longer, just in case it was what kept the looming silence at bay. For months I had used my math teacher's graduation gift to measure if there was any diminishment in the distance between the lower and upper jaw as I opened as wide as I could. The thought was that if there was the tiniest bit of difference, if the predictable locking were to occur, I would have time to announce my deception and allow my parents to take me straight to the doctor.

My grandmother said to Amy, "I remember how beautiful you looked in your fake wedding gown." Then she looked at my father. "At least, he got to see his fake grandchild," said my grandmother. Amy, seeing that her grandmother was remembering her husband, said, "Even death is a fountain, Gramma, with life at both ends."

Prouder of my father in his fake death than she was of him in life, my grandmother asked me to say something in front of the casket. "It will be cute," she said to Amy. I stood beneath my father's charts like star systems. Like clockwork. Then I recognized the fear that had been inside the nail—the fear that would lie dormant in my blood for years, maybe decades—or maybe just minutes. The hinge that was my jaw would suddenly lock up—and I would be incapable of saying the things that needed to be said.

I stood beneath my father's charts—whole rarefied ecosystems containing dots and lines and names and dates in little circles. Lyrical and threatening, they revolved slowly in the air. My mother motioned with her hand. "Go on. Say something."

THE MAJOR COMES HOME

The townspeople had forgotten what war he fought in, and it appeared even the Major couldn't recall. Though they asked him numerous times, he mumbled into the sleeve of his uniform, so it was impossible for them to make out his response. The mayor suggested we make a list of the possible wars. "So he can receive his proper recognition." The date for the parade was determined. "Just clear up this war thing, and we'll be ready to roll." The Major's medals were like blisters on his chest.

Mr. Holcolme, the history teacher, was selected as the one to supervise the task. After making a list, he asked the townspeople to respond. "If we approach this logically, thinking in terms of dates, locations, causes, possible enemies, we can certainly narrow it down." The town anxiously awaited the results as the day for the celebration approached. The Major crumpled up behind his medals, his hands pasted in his lap.

"I think we can eliminate the Boxer Rebellion," said Dr. Fiddler, who was assigned to give the Major a physical to determine his health and also to see if his body yielded any clues. "Perhaps a bayonet wound.

But we shouldn't get our hopes up too much," he said to Thump, the town sheriff.

Mr. Holcolme reminded us that the list was not in chronological order, but if we methodically approached the issue, we could determine with a degree of certitude in which war the Major fought. "Until that time," said the mayor, "he should be treated as a hero and accorded all the privileges . . . one would ordinarily accord a man of his . . . accomplishments and . . . demeanor."

We knew the Major, crushed behind the weight of his medals, was going to be old, but no one suspected he would appear as old as he did.

His medals sparkled threateningly.

Mr. Holcolme saw history as a series of concealments and subterfuges. Why something happened was essentially an enigma, but it was always connected to other enigmas, and that was the point of history, recognizing the subtleties of those connections. The students, noisy and shallow, never sensed the rotting that went on behind the maps of his classroom walls. The students had no respect for the power that could alter everything. Tyrants. Genocide. The threat of mass destruction. In the past, that used to get people's attention. "I specialize in what everybody else wants to forget," Mr. Holcolme announced the first day of class, while the students numbly endured him. That was when he first saw Cindy sitting at her desk like dew.

When Brendan wasn't sick, he'd sit in Mr. Holcolme's class and gaze at Cindy, who sat two rows in front of him. Mr. Holcolme in a corduroy jacket paced back and forth, brandishing a pointer he jabbed at pastel countries hung from tacks. Cindy in a chalk-colored sundress sat above history, even above time.

Brendan never let her see him looking, catching glimpses of her while he doodled in the back of a notebook. Feeling that whatever he wrote about was somehow damaged, he never wrote about Cindy.

Instead, he wrote about his father's red, threatening eyes.

The barber indicated that the Major would have a lifetime's worth of free haircuts. He said to Thump, "You know, I saw a man digging holes the other day, and another man kept coming up behind him, filling the holes back up with dirt."

"Town workers?" asked Thump. He could feel the scissors clicking around his ears.

"Yeah. They said the man who put in the trees called in sick."

Though no one in the town remembered the Major's family, everyone was assured they were upright, noble, and patriotic. "All the members of his family were unwavering in their support," said the mayor in the speech he delivered the day of the celebration. But ultimately no one was sure whether they died or just moved away. Whether they were respectable or feared. Whether they were important or just like everybody else.

And then Billy Waddles, the owner of the gas station, claimed he was a second cousin.

"You are not a second cousin," declared Walter, the retired insurance man.

"How do you know?" asked Billy. "I could be a second cousin."

"How many haircuts can a bald man ask for?" Thump asked Walter, who sipped his warm beer in Pudge's.

Everybody looked forward to the big parade to celebrate the Major coming home. People named their children after him, and not to be outdone, those who had older children renamed them. Billy Waddles said he would give the Major a full tank of gas every week for as long as the Major lived. Of course, the Major didn't drive, but everyone appreciated the offer. "That's the least I can do for a relative."

"You are not a second cousin," Walter grunted as cigarette smoke curled around his fingers.

Mr. Holcolme said he had devised a way to identify in which war the Major fought. The mayor and Thump met with the Major in Dr. Fiddler's office. They were to determine the Major's reaction to a list of words based on the assumption that a soldier would always hate his enemy. Each of them would indicate a nationality, and based on the Major's "level of disgust," they would be able to determine precisely in which war he had fought.

However, the experiment failed when it was determined that the Major reacted negatively to each nationality.

"Maybe he's a veteran of a lot of wars," said Thump.

"Based on this, he'd have to be a veteran of every war that was ever fought—and even a lot we haven't fought," said Mr. Holcolme.

When Dr. Fiddler removed the blood pressure cup from the thin arm of the Major, the rip sound startled him.

"Which should give us even more reason to honor him," said the mayor.

"Right," said Thump.

Brendan's mother, Debbie, was a hairdresser who spent her whole life inside the cloud of hair on women's heads, and she perpetually smelled of chemicals—dyes and permanents. They saturated her clothes, her skin, her house. Brendan never knew the real color of his mother's hands. "I work with their hair," she said to Brendan, "but I really put hope inside their heads."

Her husband, who had once played football with Thump, had been laid off for almost a year.

"I don't want to hear none of that. There's nobody I'd rather have in the trenches with me," said Thump to Debbie when she said she and her husband were having problems.

Brendan had given up trying to be like everybody else. He loved the days he was home sick with his mother—but now his father was there, and he had never missed a day of school. Brendan felt the disappointment every time he looked in his father's eyes. Brendan watched Cindy from a distance.

When Mr. Holcolme asked Cindy questions about history, about a general or a city or a battle or a plague, Brendan would will her the answer, and she would always get it right, though she never really understood that Brendan was responsible.

Mr. Holcolme once said to Walter, "I can't bear to tell her she's wrong."

Thump had once been the quarterback for the high school team, the year they had a losing record, and he spent the season being collapsed on in the pocket. He had volunteered for the armed forces right out of high school and spent time in a war everybody refused to acknowledge because we didn't win. After spending several years working for the town on the road crew and after several more working for the plastic plant, he became the town sheriff. He told Walter, the retired insurance man, that only he knew what the Major was going through. "Imagine the disappointment. After the surge of power and fear. Imagine coming back here. After your arteries have been opened up, after your head has had a flash of light inside it, it ain't easy to settle on this." His eyes were dark and tiny, like the tops of carpet tacks.

The maps of the world fell off Mr. Holcolme's classroom walls. He painstakingly observed the movements of the past. Who could pry up all the secrets? The countries like amoebas rubbing their backs together.

A. History is a thief of time.

B. History is memory stuck in a trap.

C. History has abandoned us.

Brendan tried to will Cindy the correct answer, but he didn't know which one was right.

Brendan's father had been laid off from the plastic plant. His mother viewed the Major's arrival as a sign that perhaps things were going to be better. She subscribed to travel magazines and always imagined her suitcase was packed and she was headed for someplace else—a piazza, a shop, a terrace, a ballroom.

She had purchased a set of American Tourister luggage when she was single though, she had never used them. They were the color of sky and water and the color of destination.

Some places had floating qualities, and that's where she wanted to be.

Walter would sit at Pudge's and look through the obituaries. "We have to invent a few heroes."

"Why?" asked Pudge.

"So we know who to blame when things don't go the way we want them." Walter leaned on his elbows over a flat beer.

He was full of benign contempt and terminal dismay.

If you said it was hot, he'd say it was the humidity. If you said it was cold, he'd say it was the wind factor.

His cigarette burned away in the ashtray. "Just cause I gave up smoking them, doesn't mean I don't like the smell," he'd say.

His greatest debates issued out of the difference between whole life and term.

"What about a free policy for the Major?" asked Pudge.

"I'm retired," said Walter.

"It's a mood thing," said Dr. Fiddler to Brendan's mother. "Nothing serious."

"But he just sits there. He don't say anything. He don't want anything. He just has hate in his eyes. It just seems that he's going to kill somebody."

"Keep him home. Away from anybody he could hurt. And he'll be fine."

"What about me?"

The doctor interlocked his plump fingers. "Don't irritate him . . . with obligations . . . with complaints."

She remembered what her fingers felt beneath her mother's hair—a terrible dark.

Pudge said to Thump, "I just heard old Dr. Fiddler named a procedure after the Major."

The smoke from Walter's cigarette billowed from the ashtray.

"What's that?" asked Cash.

"Calls it Major surgery," said Pudge, and he stuck a coaster under a glass of beer.

Brendan's father, his eyes with more radish-red where there should have been more white, said to Brendan's mother before he stopped talking, "Why do you read all those travel books? It will only make you think there is someplace else." Debbie was silent. These were the kind of conversations that usually ended with her husband telling her that she was to blame for the fact that things were not better.

She looked at her travel books. Placid hotel rooms waited at the end.

Mr. Holcolme announced to the mayor, "Given the ambiguous drabness of his uniform, and the indecipherable messages on the medals, there is the distinct possibility he never served for our military at all. In addition, he may have even fought for the other side."

"What does that mean?" asked the mayor. "The other side? The other side of what?"

In the controversy that ensued, Mr. Holcolme was removed from his teaching position. He was accused of "lascivious behavior."

"What does that mean?" asked Mr. Holcolme. "Remember the story of the Trojan Horse," he warned as he was escorted from his desk and its pile of toppling books.

"Don't worry about the maps. You can come back later for them," said the mayor.

Brendan regretted having written about Mr. Holcolme in the back of his notebook. Deciding not to write in it again, he stuck it inside his mother's suitcase.

Half of the women in the town said to Debbie, "Don't put up with it."

And the other half said, "At least, you got a man."

The minister picked a piece of lint off the shoulder of her blue suit. "Sometimes you just need to count your blessings," she said.

On the day of the celebration for the Major, the barber stood with his scissors clicking to the beat of the school band. The parade was life itself—multifaceted and scary—the whole thing jerking along, jolting forward as if all the disparate parts were connected with pieces of string.

Because it didn't require a great deal of musical ability, and it gave him an opportunity to be around Cindy, Brendan played the cymbals in the band.

His mother told him she had a surprise for him after the ceremonies.

The parade advanced. The scouts with their merit badges and rolled-up pants scooted down the street while the fire department seriously marched. Didda-one. Didda-one. Didda-onetwothree. The fire truck was the color of Cindy's nail polish. The redness of the truck splattered into the shop windows. The bicycles wobbled with crepe paper tied to handlebars and wrapped around the spokes of the wheels. The car containing the minister, the priest, the mayor, and the doctor advanced cautiously.

Autumn colors fell down in the back of the town.

"He's going to catch pneumonia," said the barber as the Major, huddled up and sleeping, passed in the convertible.

Cindy's baton tumbled through the town's sky.

Tiny silver beads sparkled from her white boots while the drummer's drumsticks pecked out a marching rhythm.

The parade moved like an ocean liner.

Proudly leading them through the streets, Cindy was a piece of kinetic energy at the prow of the parade.

The Major Comes Home

The band played a musical tribute to all the branches of the military, and it included all the patriotic rat-a-tat-tat and all the trumpet blare associated with every war they could think of—just in case.

Brendan's cymbals flashed like two gold suns.

As Cindy spun and kicked her legs, the music flowed behind her. Mr. Holcolme, standing in the back of the crowd with a bag of maps, felt her flickering inside his head.

The drummers knocked out a military march.

The countries in Mr. Holcolme's bag were like paint flakes.

The tuba players dug the music out of their instruments. The trumpet players lifted a golden sound out of their mouths. The street was on fire as the trombones blazed in the autumn sun. Cindy high kicked and dragged the music down the street.

Then the parade came to a halt in front of the platform that had been constructed in the center of the town. The band members, with feather dusters attached to their hats, stood uncomfortably erect. The instruments knelt like gold stumps beside the tuba players.

Several weeks before, Debbie had gone to Walter, the retired insurance man. "What kind of disability is that?" Walter asked. "Depression? You just go to work sad—like everybody else. You just live your life with a big chunk of sorrow stuck inside you—like everybody else. Disability insurance for sadness? I mean, everybody would have to collect it."

The woman who owned Bede's Restaurant named a hamburger after the Major. Her cheeks plump like hamburger buns—her mouth a smudge of dried ketchup.

Debbie felt the flutter of memory beneath the women's scalps. Every Saturday she visited the nursing home and did her mother's tender gray helmet of hair. She touched her where her past was buried. Her mother hadn't called her Debbie in years.

"Mom, it's me. Debbie," she'd say. And her mother, sitting inside a sour smell, would ask her to leave.

The town wanted to give the Major an award—a trophy, some commemorative artifact that would capture the day's significance. They couldn't think of anything appropriate. Then they decided on the parade, some speeches, and finally a spectacular performance by Cindy.

Thump helped the Major from the convertible to his place of honor on the platform. It was as if someone had stuck the Major inside a uniform and now he had to decide what it meant—whether it represented a side and if, indeed, that was truly the side he was on. He looked as if he were still making up his mind. He fingered a button as if he were surprised.

The minister ran through her speech:

1. Grace of God

2. Biblical story

The priest ran through his speech

1. Biblical story

2. Grace of God

Together they were responsible for the town's soul, except for the soul of Walter, who clung stubbornly to his belief in whole life.

Their voices creaked as the Major sat on stage—achingly thin, slightly slumped, hand on chest, as if he were holding the hole inside himself. The priest coughed sanctimoniously into a handkerchief. The minister wondered why he had called her hat godly.

The Major Comes Home

Walter imagined the platform on the verge of collapse. He imagined the lawsuits, the claims. He thought how unfair people are for taking advantage of a situation.

"If you imagine something is going to happen, it doesn't," Walter would say to Pudge. "So that's why it is good to imagine things like being struck by lightning. Don't ever imagine winning a lottery."

"Or touching Cindy's skin," said Mr. Holcolme.

The priest spoke about the Major's service to God and his country. He talked about Saint Gall driving a blackbird from a girl's pink mouth. "Do not think that I have come to bring peace on earth; I have not come to bring peace, but a sword."

The minister spoke about the Major's service to his country and to God. "The lion shall eat straw with the ox; and dust shall be the serpent's food," she said.

The priest wondered why the minister had thanked him, and he thought he probably shouldn't have mentioned the gaudiness of her hat, but it did seem inappropriate on such an occasion.

Earlier in the week, Dr. Fiddler, fat and disheveled, had examined the Major and discovered a hole in his chest. It wasn't really a wound. It was far more disturbing than a wound. It wasn't as if something—a bullet or a piece of shrapnel—had gone in and dug around inside. Rather, it was as if something had been pulled out. It didn't look like a wound—ragged, sore, and moist. It didn't even look like a healed wound. It resembled a porthole. It was more like a root hole. "You can close your shirt now," said the doctor, almost embarrassed.

Then the mayor spoke: "We owe him everything. All the deeds he performed were done in our name—no matter how courageous or how disturbing, no matter how noble or crazy. No matter how many lives were irrevocably altered because of him, shattered even. Our lives are better because he did the things that he had to do. We would not be here today without his sacrifice. Our way of life has been preserved."

The mayor talked about our resolve, our determination to be victorious, our vigor, and our freedom. "It all comes down to freedom," he said. And the crowd obligingly applauded.

Billy Waddles turned to Walter. "You got to admit the Major does look a lot like me."

The French horns hung like golden tumors from the bodies of the band members.

Mr. Holcolme had snuck in behind the crowd. He had just come from his classroom and carried his maps in a paper bag. As he stood waiting for Cindy's performance, he thought of the way beauty is reckless and defiant. Contemptuous. Beauty is a force. It shifts boundaries. It paralyzes whole worlds. It devastates. Beauty has no mercy. Only beauty has the power to change the world, and that isn't a good thing. "If you want to know what history feels like," he said to his students, "drop an anvil on your foot."

He had looked at his maps before he packed them up. What fed beneath the surface? What sucked the colors out of the countries? Beauty, he thought.

Sure, you can be on the lookout for all that is bad, but how can we protect ourselves from beauty?

"Maybe he's already killed something," Dr. Fiddler had said to Debbie.

"What do you mean?"

"In his mind."

The Major gave Debbie hope—like you could go through something terrible and come out the other end. A waking up was inside her. Morning waited on the other side.

As Cindy walked to the center of the platform, Thump stood tensely off to the side. Nobody can understand what it is like, he thought, as he stared at the Major.

The man whose job was to place the trees in the holes leaned close to the platform.

"We are in for a special treat," said the mayor.

Cindy produced a baton with both ends wrapped in gauze, which she dipped into a bucket of lighter fluid. Then Thump struck a kitchen match on his belt, cupped it in his hands till it flared, and lit both ends of the baton. The scouts, plastered in merit, dutifully watched.

While the Major appeared to be slightly agitated, with his medals slapped against his chest, the band members stood in rows. When Brendan looked over his shoulder, he was startled to see his father, standing with two suitcases, his eyes drilling holes in the crowd. Time moved more slowly, more dangerously, around his father's hands.

When she said good-bye to her mother that morning, Debbie had her fingers inside her mother's hair. When she saw her husband standing with the packed suitcases, her heart almost knocked her over.

While the Major, clutching at a sunken space beneath his uniform, sat transfixed by memory or vision, Cindy's nails, the color of an emergency, artfully jabbed the air. Brendan knew she would be spectacular. She twirled, celestially and powerfully, before she tossed the baton into the sky, so it flickered above her, starlike, spinning wildly—a detachable part of her, mesmerizing, unreachable, forever unknowable. The whole town was silent except for Brendan's father, who, holding up the suitcases, bellowed from the back of the crowd.

When Brendan saw his father's red eyes and the contents of the suitcases, his mother's travel books and his notebook, spilling in the street, he flashed together his cymbals. And the sound that came out of metal slapping against metal jarred the molecules that held the town together, startled corpuscles, jolted atoms, loosened the grip of gravity.

The baton burned above us suspended for what seemed like forever, but, if it were forever, the town knew this represented hope. It would take another forever for it to fall.

Acknowledgments

Northwest Review, The Bitter Oleander, Fiction '83, Nexus, Stone Canoe, and *Salt Hill.*

I would like to thank Martha Rhodes, Ryan Murphy, Martha Carlson-Bradley and Sally Ball for their critical contribution in helping to place my voice inside these pages. And I would like to thank Molly LaCroix for putting my face on this book. And a special thanks to Robert and Shana ParkeHarrison for allowing their beautiful image to appear on the cover.

Thanks to the numerous fiction writers who encouraged me and believed a poet could write stories—Phil LeMarche, Mary Ann Cain, Paul Griner, Kirsten Kaschok, Ryan Ridge, and Ashley Farmer. And thanks for the friendship, support, and spiritual energy from George Kalamaras, Paul Roth, Linda Tomol Penissi, David Lloyd, Michael Burkard, and Jeffrey Ethan Lee. My work would not be what it is without their love and influence.

I'm grateful for the many colleagues and friends at the colleges where I've taught (Onondaga Community College, Syracuse University, SUNY College of Environmental Science and Forestry, and LeMoyne). As always the students at these colleges inspire me daily. And, of course, I wish to offer abundant thanks to my family—for all we have endured and dreamed. Throughout we have laughed and loved.

Thanks to all those who taught me that stories live in poems and poems live in stories.

Patrick Lawler lives in Syracuse, New York. He is the author of five collections of poetry: *A Drowning Man Is Never Tall Enough* (University of Georgia Press, 1990), *reading a burning book* (Basfal Books, 1994), *Feeding the Fear of the Earth* (Many Mountains Moving Press, 2006), *Trade World Center* (Ravenna Press, 2012), and *Underground (Notes Toward an Autobiography)*—which combines an interview with poetry and memoir (Many Mountains Moving Press, 2011). His novel, *Rescuers of Skydivers Search Among the Clouds,* is the winner of the Ronald Sukenick American Book Review Innovative Fiction Prize of Fiction Collective 2 (University of Alabama Press, 2012). The Bitter Oleander Press will be publishing his poetry book *Child Sings in the Womb* (2014). Lawler is the recipient of numerous awards and fellowships, including a National Endowment for the Arts fellowship, two New York State Foundation for the Arts grants, a Saltonstall Artist's grant, and a CNY Book Award for Fiction. At SUNY College of Environmental Science and Forestry, he teaches literature of nature and environmental writing courses, and he is writer in residence at LeMoyne College where, besides poetry and fiction, he teaches scriptwriting and playwriting.